## BOOKS BY ELLEN HOWARD

*Circle of Giving*

*When Daylight Comes*

*Gillyflower*

*Edith Herself*

*Her Own Song*

*Sister*

*The Chickenhouse House*

*The Cellar*

*The Tower Room*

*A Different Kind of Courage*

*The Gate in the Wall*

# ELLEN HOWARD

THE GATE in the WALL

F
HOW

A JEAN KARL BOOK

ATHENEUM BOOKS for YOUNG READERS

ACKNOWLEDGMENTS

With gratitude to Christine Wasche of the Macclesfield
Museums Trust and to Black Prince Holidays
and Napton Narrowboats.

Atheneum Books for Young Readers
An imprint of Simon & Schuster Children's Publishing Division
1230 Avenue of the Americas
New York, New York 10020

Book design by Michael Nelson
The text of this book is set in Horley Old Style

Printed in the United States of America
10 9 8 7 6 5 4 3 2 1

Library of Congress Cataloging-in-Publication Data
Howard, Ellen.
The gate in the wall / Ellen Howard.—1st ed.
p. cm.
"A Jean Karl book"
Summary: In nineteenth-century England, ten-year-old Emma, accustomed
to long working hours at the silk mill and the poverty and hunger of her sis-
ter's house, finds her life completely changed when she inadvertently gets a
job on a canal boat carrying cargoes between several northern towns.
ISBN 0-689-82295-2
[1. Canals—Fiction. 2. Children—Employment—Fiction. 3. Orphans—
Fiction. 4. England—Fiction.] I. Title.
PZ7.H83274Gat 1999
[Fic]—dc21 98-22250

FIRST
**F**
EDITION

*For Chuck, "O Captain! My Captain!"*

# CONTENTS

| | | |
|---|---|---|
| 1 | THE GATE | 1 |
| 2 | MRS. MINSHULL | 9 |
| 3 | DRIVIN' ROSIE | 16 |
| 4 | THE CANAL | 25 |
| 5 | WORK | 31 |
| 6 | *CYGNET*'S HUFFLER | 39 |
| 7 | FLOWERS IN THE DUST | 47 |
| 8 | MANCHESTER | 55 |
| 9 | BOOTS AND BONNET | 62 |
| 10 | GETTIN' AHEAD | 70 |
| 11 | A LIGHT IN THE DARK | 78 |
| 12 | BIRDIE | 87 |
| 13 | THE WALL | 95 |
| 14 | NANCY | 103 |
| 15 | FLINCHIN' | 109 |
| 16 | JOCK NEVINS | 116 |
| 17 | PAIN | 124 |
| 18 | HINDRANCE | 130 |
| 19 | . . . AND JOY | 138 |
| | GLOSSARY | 147 |

"If you wish to be changed, find a gate."

—Mary Scriver,
*Sweetgrass and Cottonwood Smoke*

# ~ To the Reader ~

For almost two hundred years, from the opening of the Newry Canal in 1745 until the end of World War II, the British canal system was an important highway for the transport of goods. Built when roads in England were virtually nonexistent, there were more than five thousand miles of canals and navigable rivers in Great Britain during the boom time of canal boat transport in the late eighteenth and early nineteenth centuries.

*A typical canal boat*

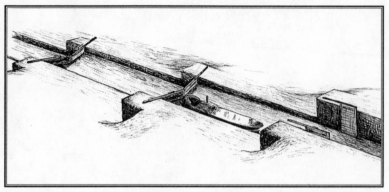

*A canal boat in a flight of double-wide locks.*

The origin of the unique culture of the people who lived and worked on canal boats is obscured in mystery. For the most part, canal boat folk lived ignored by the larger civilization. Unschooled in all but the skills of their difficult livelihoods, they were born, worked, married, raised families, and died on their narrowboats, in cabins only ten feet long, seven feet wide, and five feet high. In many ways, it was a life as circumscribed as the limits of their boats, but canal folk developed an ethic, a language, a mode of dress and decoration, and a body of art that gave their lives grace. Compared to other British working-class people of their time, the English canal boat folk created for themselves a world of beauty and freedom.

#  The Gate

She had passed it, morn and night, the three years since she was taken on at the silk mill—a low wooden gate in the high brick wall that snaked beside the street. But always before, it had been shut fast and barred with an iron bolt. Emma had not even known she saw the gate until now, when it stood open.

She leaned against the wall to still the trembling of her legs. Her belly clenched hard with hunger, and she remembered she had not eaten before she left the cottage. It was no wonder, with all the mithering of that morning to distract her.

First it had been the baby, scorching its hand among the coals and setting up a screech. Emma supposed it had crawled into the fireplace, seeking a bit of warmth. But its screeching had wakened her older sister, Nancy, who had cried aloud with a mother's sharp fear at the hurting of her child. The hurt was slight, as Emma had seen when she grabbed the baby from the ashes. But by then, Ben too had wakened. He came up off his pallet on the floor with curses and blows for all in his way.

"Canna a man get a wink o' sleep by his own hearthside?" he had roared, lamming Nancy so she staggered and almost dropped the baby. Emma had taken it from her and retreated to a corner while Nancy soothed her husband. He would not miss his sleep so dearly had he not spent half the night at the public house, swilling gin with his cronies, Emma had thought.

"Just run 'round the corner, sister dear," Nancy had whispered when Ben subsided onto the only chair, nursing his head in his hands. "Get threepenny-worth o' brandy to warm his tea."

She had pressed coins—their last, Emma knew—into Emma's hand and taken the baby back.

But the nearest public house was not yet open, it was so early. The streets were dead dark and silent, and Emma had trudged farther, to the Buxton Road, where factory hands were beginning to appear on their way to work.

So should *I* be on me way, Emma had fretted, making her purchase in an unfamiliar inn and hurrying toward home. Nancy met her at the door, her finger pressed to her lips. Emma had scarcely paused, for by then the streets were emptying again, the workers gone to the mills. She had a long walk before her, so she clutched her shawl about her shoulders and ran. There was a stitch in her side, and her breath came fast when at last she saw the mill door, with Mr. Jakes standing by it, his great gold watch in his hand. Emma knew he had seen her, and still he turned his back, slow and deliberate, and walked through the door, pulling it fast behind him.

Emma had flung herself upon the door, just as it closed, beating it with her fists.

"If ye please, Mr. Jakes," she had called, sobbing. "I be but a minute late!"

But the door had remained shut, deaf and mute to her cries. She was locked out for the day, and her pay would be docked. What would Ben say when she came again home and the day not yet begun?

Now Emma straightened slowly from the wall where she leaned and brushed back the hair from her eyes. She'd not had the chance to tidy herself this morning, and she could feel how her hair straggled on her neck and see how disordered was her dress. She smoothed her apron with her hands and tucked the ends of her shawl into the waistband. Her bare feet were bespattered with street filth, and she thought to wash them when she got home, if the water in the courtyard tap was running. She took a deep breath, pushing down the tremor of fear that rose when she thought of home. Perhaps Ben would be out by the time she got there. Perhaps she might earn a penny or two this day helping old Maeve, the washerwoman, with her tubs. Perhaps . . .

Emma forced herself to take a step away from the shelter of the wall and toward home. Another step and she was passing the gate. . . .

He would lam her. Emma knew it, though she tried not to think of it. He would lam her as he often lammed Nancy, until she fell down, and if his temper was foul—how could it not be foul after such an awakening?—he would kick her when she was down. Emma faltered, her ribs aching already from the imagined blows. She peered through the open gate.

The dawn light glinted off of something. . . . Was it water there beyond the wall? A pond or a stream mayhap?

In all her many journeyings to and from the mill, Emma had never taken thought of what might lie behind this high brick wall. But now, her heart pounding with dread of what awaited her at home, she paused once again and craned to see through the gateway. The gate, its paint scarred by the mischief of boys, swung free on its hinges; and thick about the gateway grew bushes, misted with the new green of spring. Through the green branches glinted the water, silver gleams in the dawn light.

Would the lamming be any the harder for coming late, Emma wondered as she stepped through the gateway.

Here, on the other side of the wall, where houses did not press so close about, Emma was suddenly aware of the sky, colorless and clear. This seemed almost a country place, with the new fresh thicket all about her. Perhaps she might find some greens for Nancy to boil for Ben's dinner. That might soften him.

The path was not much used. Emma could tell by the branches arching low across it and by the untrampled wisps of new grass that grew along its course. She pushed toward the glint of water. Though it was but a few steps, the going was hard, with the branches whipping into her eyes. She shoved forward and felt herself break free of the thicket about the gate. She shook her head to clear her hair of twigs and opened her squinted eyes.

Before her lay the water, a placid ribbon of it between stone banks. The sun broke over the horizon and turned its surface to gold, dazzling Emma's eyes.

But even more dazzling was what lay upon the water. It was a boat, long and narrow, with its black hull riding low. A tarpaulin was tented across its cargo for most of its length, but at one end was a tiny cabin, topped by a black stovepipe. Emma had never seen such color as glowed from that cabin!

She ventured toward it, her head tilted wonderingly to one side. There was red and yellow and green and blue, diamonds and stripes and curlicues of color. There was writing too, on the side of the cabin. Painfully, Emma spelled out the letters, a great lot of them, arching above and below a small round brass-bound window curtained with lace. They seemed to Emma wondrously formed, picked out in gold against a deep blue background, with flowers painted about them as bright and fresh as though they had been just gathered from a garden. Emma wished she knew what the letters signified, but though she went to school most Sundays when Nancy did not need her at home, she could read only little words—"bun" and "run" and such.

Emma wandered slowly along the edge of the water and gazed at the paintwork of the boat, at the white coils of rope, at the black water cans—painted also with roses and diamonds and stripes—that sat on the roof alongside a mop and two long painted poles. There was writing on the black hull of the boat also, she saw: C-Y-G-N-E-T.

Emma wrinkled her nose at a familiar earthy smell. Her stomach griped with hunger, and she recognized the smell—potatoes. Was that the boat's cargo?

She shot a quick glance up and down the stream and back along the short path to the thicket-edged wall. No one. Swiftly, she knelt and forced her hand beneath the tight-lashed tarpaulin. Her hand met a familiar rounded shape, and she drew forth a potato. Her heart was beating in her throat, fast and painful. Surely the boatman would not miss one, out of so many! She scampered to the shelter of the thicket and crouched, gnawing at the raw potato.

It would have been tastier had she been able to boil it or roast it in coals; but raw potato was better than nothing, Emma thought, wiping the dirt from her mouth when she had finished. What a slattern I be, she thought, ashamed suddenly that she had not taken thought to wash it, with so much water to hand. How Nancy would gladden to be able to dip her kettle into so much water, brown though it was, Emma thought. It was more than she could do to keep house and the baby's clothes washed, with the tap in the courtyard so seldom turned on. And how she would relish a nice potato! Indeed, an apronful of potatoes would sweeten even Ben's temper. Only where could Emma say she had got them?

"We may be clemmed an' ragged," Ben often said, "but we be honest folk for a' that."

Emma crept again toward the boat, thinking hard. There was still no one in sight, though on the other side of the wall, she knew, the street would be waking—the merchants throwing open their shutters and the housewives venturing out and the children playing in the gutters.

She found herself noticing things she had not seen before. There was a path running alongside the stream, well trodden and littered with horse droppings. An arched stone bridge spanned the water in the distance. The stream itself was not like those she had played beside on the rare summer days when she was small that Father and Mother had taken the children to the country. Instead of shallow, muddy banks, this one was walled with square-cut stones, and the water was deep enough for the boat to be brought within inches of the side. It was tied to iron rings, she saw, set into the stones at intervals.

She examined the cargo space of the boat once again and saw that the tarpaulin was stretched over a line of planks, supported by stout posts, which ran from a painted triangular board at the end—was it the front or the back of the boat?—to the cabin. The tarpaulin was lashed to the planks with ropes, but was loose next to the cabin. It would be an easy matter to crawl beneath in order to fill her apron.

She stood hesitating—"We be honest folk," Ben's voice echoed in her mind—when she heard shouts from beyond the bridge, around a curve in the stream. She saw the prow of a boat nose beneath the bridge, coming swiftly toward her, it seemed to Emma. Startled, she scrambled over the side, diving under the canvas and into the hold of the boat.

# MRS. MINSHULL

At once the boat was rocking, banging gently against the stone bank. Had *she* set it in motion, she wondered, crouching in the dim hold. She made out a sleeping pallet hard by piles of sacks, full of potatoes, she knew. A few had spilled from a broken sack. It was one of those she must have eaten, Emma thought. But now the rocking of the boat unsettled her stomach, and the potato smell was sickening. The shouting voice drew nearer, and she heard the sound of a horse's hooves on the stony dirt of the path. She crept onto the pallet, closing her eyes as though that would hide her—though she knew she could not be seen beneath the tarpaulin—and clutching her stomach.

"'Tis *Cygnet*," she heard a man's voice cry. "Pass over, luv, pass over." His voice lifted. "Are ye about, Mrs. Minshull?" Then he was talking again to his companion on the bank. "'Tis peculiar, 'tis, so late of a morn, and her not gettin' ahead."

Emma heard the slither of rope on the cabin roof, then a sharp little slap, and the slither again. The rope slid the length of the plank-supported tarpaulin.

"Most like she stepped to the shops," said a woman's comfortable voice from the bank. Emma put her hands over her head, trying to make herself small, as she felt the other boat slide past.

"Rosie as well?" Already the man's voice was retreating into the distance with the passing boat. Emma listened as the clop of the horse's hooves grew faint. The rocking calmed.

But still Emma did not move from the pallet nor open her eyes. Now she felt sick, indeed, with so close an escape. She laid her cheek on the blanket beneath her and let out a trembling breath. She could hear the almost silent sounds of the water licking at the bottom of the boat. Somewhere on the bank a bird trilled suddenly, and beyond the wall, she knew, were the busy street noises of the town, though she could scarcely hear them. After her fright, the peace seemed to enfold her. The weak sunlight shone through a space at the end of the tented tarpaulin above her and warmed one foot and ankle. She moved her other foot into the warmth and pulled the blanket—a good, thick warm one, she noticed, and not dirty either—over her shoulder. It was like being rocked in Mother's arms, she thought, in the days when she was a little one, before she was sent to the mill to work from sunup to sundown. The realization swept over her that today was a holiday for her—no work, nor school either. No deafening clatter of spinning machines; no hot, noisome air to breathe. Emma relaxed her stiff shoulders and breathed in deeply the unaccustomed luxury of idleness.

"Tom! Tom Fallows, where be ye?"

At the same moment that Emma heard the shrill calling voice, she felt a small lurch of the boat. Startled, she realized that someone had stepped aboard the boat on the other side of the cabin. There was a scraping, a banging, a jostling.

Then, "Tom, ye scamp, be ye slugabed still?"

A small door in the back wall of the cabin flung open, and Emma, jerking up, was looking into a pair of sky blue eyes. They peered out at her from the brown wrinkles of a face so dark and wizened that it looked like a withered apple.

"Why, ye be not Tom!" the apple-face was screeching, and a scrawny black-clad arm shot out and grasped Emma's shoulder with clawlike fingers.

"Who be ye?" the apple-face demanded. "Who be ye? And where's Tom go to? We mun be gettin' the boat ahead!"

Emma was so astonished that she could but gape. Who *was* this old woman? Who was Tom? Then she knew—the boatman had come back, except that it was a boat*woman*, and she, Emma, was still on the boat. She had been lying here in a dream when she'd meant only to nick a few potatoes and be away home.

Home. At the same moment that she was shrugging

her shoulder from the old woman's grasp, she felt dread, like sickness, settle into the pit of her stomach.

"Speak up, lass," the old woman said, reaching to fling back a section of tarpaulin to let in more light. "What's yer business on the *Cygnet*, and where be Tom?"

"I dinna know where yer Tom may be," Emma muttered. She looked through the opening in the canvas, sighting back along the path, gauging the distance. Jump up, spring over the side, and run for home, she told herself. But she only sat, as though stupefied, while the woman squinted at her with an evil look.

"Up to na good, by the look o' ye," she said. She was a tiny hunchbacked old woman in a rusty black dress and bonnet, no taller than Emma herself. She turned over a bucket standing hard by and sat herself down, still surveying Emma with her piercing eyes.

Emma was suddenly painfully aware of her dirty face and hands and feet, of her ragged shawl and straggling hair. She drew herself up and tried to straighten her dress. She could feel those sharp eyes boring into her.

"Ye dinna see a lad hereabouts?" the woman said. "A lad so high"—she raised a knobby brown hand—"wi' straw-colored hair and a wicked look to his eye?"

Emma shook her head.

"Buggered off, I'll be bound," the old woman said. "Buggered off whilst I be gettin' Rosie shod. The rogue were ne'er worth his victuals." Then a thought seemed to strike her. "How shall I get ahead wi' none to drive th'animal? Were it not fer that, I'd be well shut o' him."

She squinted into the distance somewhere beyond Emma's shoulder. Emma stole a glance at her, and it seemed the wrinkles in her face had deepened and the blue eyes had almost disappeared into them. The woman sighed and put a hand to her chin. Her mouth was deeply sunken between it and her hooked nose. Emma guessed she hadn't many teeth. She seemed the oldest creature that Emma'd ever seen.

"An' ye, me lass," she said suddenly, making Emma start. "Ye havena said what ye be doin' on me boat."

Emma hung her head and did not answer.

"Clemmed, were ye?" the old woman said slyly, peering sidewise at her. "Mayhappen ye havena supped o' late?"

Emma felt the heaviness of the stolen potato in her stomach. "I mun be gettin' home," she muttered, half rising.

In a trice, her arm was imprisoned in the old woman's strong grip. Emma sank back in surrender, and the biting fingers loosened. The old woman rubbed the wiry gray hairs on her chin. Emma began once again to measure with her eyes the distance she must flee.

"Ye have a name?"

Again Emma jumped.

"Emma," she said. "Emma Deane."

"How many o' me taters have ye stolen, Emma Deane?"

"None!" said Emma, her voice sounding too loud.

"None, be it?" The old woman's hand shot out, flicking something from Emma's cheek. A bit of potato peel?

"Be these 'none' in yer belly, or in yer apron pocket, Emma Deane?"

"None," Emma protested again, forcing herself to look the woman in the eye. "I dinna take yer taters."

"Did ye na, Emma Deane?" the old woman said, and then she said nothing further, only leaned forward, fixing Emma with her gaze until Emma could look at her no longer and lowered her eyes.

"Ye shall have to pay fer them taters."

"Nay!" said Emma. "I will na pay fer what I have na taken!" But even as she said it, she could feel the earthy taste of potato rise in her mouth. Could the old woman smell it?

"If ye will na pay, ye mun work it off," the old woman said matter-of-factly. "Else I'll put the law on ye."

"Nay, please," Emma found herself pleading. "What mun I do? I can help wi' dollying if ye've wash. I can side yer cabin or . . . I be a good worker, I be. Tell me what to do!"

Emma thought that the twisting of the old woman's sunken mouth might be a grin.

"Ye can drive th'animal whilst I steer and help me shift the locks," she said, "and ye'd best step lively, me lass. The day be half gone, and I mun be gettin' the boat ahead."

The animal? Even as Emma wondered, her brain registered what her eyes had been seeing all along—a broad-backed shire horse, dappled gray, wearing what seemed to be a lacy white cap such as old women wore. The horse cropped the grass beside the path.

"I dinna know aught 'bout horses," Emma said.

"Ye dinna need know aught but to walk after her. I'll show ye the locks."

The old woman's grasp on Emma's arm had tightened once again, and Emma found herself dragged to her feet and then through the little door from which the woman had come. Straight through the cabin they went, and Emma had a muddled impression of shining and well-ordered clutter. She thought she saw patterns on the walls, roses perhaps, and then she was being dragged up a steep step and into the sunlight, to the small deck of the boat. The woman jumped nimbly from the deck to the bank, Emma in her wake, and then Emma was face-to-face with the huge horse. She shrank back and had to tilt her head to see into its startled eyes.

"This be Rosie, Emma Deane," the woman said. "She be a good steady animal. Ye'll have na mither o' her."

Emma found herself standing perilously close to the horse's great feet as, trembling, she watched the old woman hurry to the boat and begin fussing with a rope attached to the short mast. She was speaking as she stretched to reach it.

"I be Mrs. Minshull," she said.

# DRIVIN' ROSIE

AT FIRST ALL WAS CLAMOR—the clamor of Mrs. Minshull's curses and her screeched commands. The snort of the horse's breath as it strained against its load. The harsh striking of its hooves against the path, so near and loud that Emma jumped away to avoid being trampled. The clamor of Emma's heart.

But then, when the boat was gliding easily through the water, Mrs. Minshull left off cursing, and quiet fell around them like a blessing. Emma realized that it was easy to stay away from the horse's huge hooves. Hesitantly, she followed it. She was vaguely aware that the stream curved sharply away from the wall and that the countryside opened out into fields bordered by trees, though she still watched the horse carefully. Her heart slowed, and she began to hear birdsong and the rustle of grass and the murmur of the boat swimming through the water.

Once again, she seemed to fall into a dream. Perhaps it was relief after her terror of the horse. Perhaps it was the sunshine warming the crown of her head or its glitter on the water. Perhaps it was the quiet.

But in a while, through her stupor, Emma began to feel uneasy. They seemed so far from the town, from the tangle of quarreling voices, the constant clatter of traffic, the roar of machines. She turned to look behind her for the rooftops of Macclesfield, with their motley chimney pots and thick haze of smoke, but saw only the ribbon of water unwinding behind the boat. Mrs. Minshull perched in its rear—the cabin was at the back of the boat, Emma realized, with the deck behind the cabin—her hand on the great wooden tiller. She peered over the cabin roof and waved Emma forward with an irritable flap of her hand. Emma stumbled on.

Up ahead, she saw another stone bridge arching over the water like the one they had left behind. Above her the sky was blue and clear.

Her legs were tiring. Emma did not ordinarily do much walking, save to and from the mill and to the Sunday school and sometimes to the shops. Mostly she stood in one place, before her ranks of spinning reels, watching for loose ends of thread. Her legs and back often ached from standing so long—ten hours, or more if their baggin' time was shorted. Sometimes she leaned her knees against the rail to rest them, though Nancy said she musn't lest her legs grow crooked.

So now her steps flagged.

The horse slowed too and looked back at her—quizzically, it seemed to Emma. Then Mrs. Minshull's voice rang out over the water.

"Keep on, lass! Keep on!"

Emma kept on, and the horse kept on too.

Rosie. That was the horse's name. Rosie did indeed seem a good, steady animal, though too big by half, Emma thought, and silly in her tasseled lace cap, with her nose buried in a painted nose tin.

"Keeps her from stoppin' along the way fer a sup," Mrs. Minshull had explained when she showed Emma how to fasten the oat-filled tin to the horse's bridle. More like to keep her from biting, Emma had thought. The cap was to keep the flies off, Mrs. Minshull said.

But now, Emma began to think that perhaps Rosie wouldn't bite. Certainly the horse stepped skillfully along the path, placing her great feet with care away from Emma's toes. Emma ventured to come up beside her and hesitantly placed a hand on the wooden-beaded harness. The horse turned her head and fixed Emma with a calm brown gaze.

Emma wondered why she, Emma, was needed. She thought that Rosie probably knew to go along like this, pulling the boat behind her until they arrived wherever they were going. Emma hoped it wasn't far. She really must get home soon to tell Nancy what had happened that morning at the mill.

"How far?" she hollered across the water to Mrs. Minshull.

But the old woman did not seem to hear. Emma sighed. It could not be much farther, she thought.

The sun grew warmer. Emma began to notice the buzzing of bees in the hedge beside the path. Yellow flowers bloomed there, in the new grass beneath the hedge—primroses, was it, that Mother used to call them? They passed an orchard, the trees like ladies in great flowery hats of white and pink, and Emma wished she had her Sunday school slate to try to copy their graceful shapes. They came to another bridge and another.

Emma must have been walking an hour or more when she saw ahead of her, as she rounded a bend, a great stone building coming right down to the water.

It must be a mill, Emma thought. Only mills, in her experience—mills and the great St. Michael's Church in the Market Place—were built so high. Indeed, as she neared the building, Emma spelled out the letters S-I-L-K painted in white on the gray stones. That was a word she could read. Silk was what her father had come to Macclesfield to weave in the long-ago days when silk weaving meant prosperity. It was what had made Ben a fine catch—a well-paid factory engineer—when Nancy married him. And now, until Ben found work again or Nancy would consent to leave her nursing babe, silk was what Emma herself worked to keep the family in bread.

Emma stared up at the blank windows of the looming mill. She could hear the noise of the engines within. She had a sudden fear that Mr. Jakes might come striding out the tall door to shout at her. This was not *her* mill, Emma told herself. Still, she found her steps hurrying, and Rosie gave her a startled look when she tugged impatiently at the harness.

When the mill's din had receded into the distance, Emma breathed free.

The high sun burned the top of Emma's head, and she thought she could not much longer put one foot before the other when she was roused from her misery by Mrs. Minshull's voice, calling her name.

"Emma! Emma Deane!" came the cracked old voice, and looking back, Emma saw that Mrs. Minshull had steered the boat near to the bank and was holding out to her a handkerchief-wrapped packet on the end of a long pike. Emma ran back to grab the pike. By the time she had unfastened the packet, Rosie and the boat were far ahead, and Emma had to run to pass back the pike. The packet was heavy, and as she walked behind the horse, she unwrapped a meat pie and a bottle of tea.

"Thank ye kindly," she hollered back to Mrs. Minshull, who seemed to be eating her own dinner from off the cabin roof. Emma had not dreamed the old woman would feed her.

The meat pie was lovely, just such a pie as she had often longed to buy from a street vendor as she trudged home from work to a supper of kettle broth. Emma ate it gratefully. Surely they had not much farther to go, but now it did not seem so urgent to Emma to turn back. She still had plenty of time to get home before the mill let out, and Nancy would not fret until then. She felt suddenly strong with the pie in her belly, and her legs seemed to have accustomed themselves to the walking. Only the soles of her feet felt a little bruised from the stones of the path. She was not so weary, she thought, as she would be by this time in the mill, with her shoulders stiff from reaching to tie the threads, and her fingers numb, and the small of her back aching.

Twice, after she had eaten, they passed other boats, neither one so prettily painted as Mrs. Minshull's. Emma would see first the oncoming horse and the boy who drove it. Both times it *was* a boy, who nodded politely and put his horse between Rosie and the hedge. As the horses came up to each other, the other horse would halt, just for an instant, and when its line went slack, the boy would pass it over Rosie's back. Then the other horse would pull forward again, and the rope would slide quickly the length of Mrs. Minshull's boat. The first time, Emma was so surprised to see the cabin chimney tilt forward, then right itself as the rope passed over, that she forgot to be afraid of the strange horse passing by. When the second boat passed, Emma watched carefully to see how it was done, but she could not guess the trick. She wondered how it was decided who passed over and who under, and if she would know how to flip the rope just so if ever she should be the one to pass over.

Mrs. Minshull seemed to know the other boatmen, for they exchanged pleasantries, but she never left off looking where she steered.

Emma began to look forward to seeing what lay

21

beyond each curve in the stream. It might be a farm cottage, twined with vines just leafing out, or a field of cows, their black-and-white heads bent intently to the grass. She saw an early brood of ducklings, bits of brown fluff, borne along by the water as though they were drifting leaves.

At one place, Emma was astonished to realize that the stream of water was crossing a valley as though on a bridge. The path ran beside it, but she could look over the railing beside the path and see a town of stone-built houses below, with the hills crowding close around. What town was this, she wondered. Was this their destination?

Yet they went on, beneath another bridge—Emma had lost track now of how many. I must turn back, she told herself when she saw, at the edge of the town, another mill, this one built of brick. But instead, she found herself hurrying past, holding her breath against its evil smell and the smoke that belched from its chimneys.

Now, for a while, there were no towns or mills, only an occasional lonely cottage. Though every moment put yet more distance between her and home, Emma felt strangely happy. It was the greenness, and the flowers and sweet smells, she thought. She so seldom had a chance to walk in the sunshine. Despite the nagging sense that she should turn 'round, Emma felt her heart lift.

It seemed like waking from a dream when, having passed two more tiny hamlets and three more boats and innumerable bridges, Emma heard Mrs. Minshull hail her and realized that the boat was steering toward the bank. When the bow touched, Rosie stopped all on her own, and the old woman hopped onto the path, the bow rope in her hand.

"Hold fast, lass," she ordered, tossing it to Emma, and hurried to the stern, where she grabbed a coil of stern rope and pulled the boat more snugly to the bank. Then she set about pounding stakes into the grass beside the path with a heavy mallet.

"Is't here that ye were going?" Emma asked, puzzled. She could see no buildings, only the two bridges between which Mrs. Minshull was mooring the boat. Where would Mrs. Minshull unload her potatoes, and who would buy them in this lonely spot?

Mrs. Minshull snorted.

"I be going to Manchester," she said shortly, "but I've no wish to try the Marple locks wi' a fagged-out huffler. Ye'll need all yer wits about ye to shift locks, Emma Deane. Mornin's time enough."

Morning!

"I canna help ye in the morn," Emma protested. "I mun be gettin' home."

The old woman cackled.

"Home be it? Ye're a fair way from home, lass, if by home ye mean Macclesfield."

"But . . . ," stammered Emma. She knew they had come a long way, but if she started out now and hurried . . .

Mrs. Minshull was back on the boat, beckoning to her.

"Step lively now, lass," she called. "I'll see to th'animal while ye have a wash. I canna have ye sleepin' on me clean side bed in that filthy state."

Sleeping?

Emma looked back the way they had come. She had done as the old woman asked. One day's work would have to suffice to pay for the potato. Nancy would be dateless with worry were she not home by dark. . . .

It was then that Emma admitted to herself what she had known all along. The sun hung low in the sky. The shadows of hedges and trees were long on the grass. Her body was weary.

It *is* too late to go home this day, she confessed to herself. I'll set off in the morn.

# THE CANAL

"STEP BELOW and shed yer togs, Emma Deane," said Mrs. Minshull. "I've boiled the water, and there be a can of cold and plenty of soap. I shall have to pick out yer hair, I'll be bound, and dose ye wi' fleabane. But I mun see to Rosie first."

Just as Mrs. Minshull said, there was a copper tea-kettle of hot water hung before the flame of the bottle-shaped stove inside the cabin door. A water can of cold stood on the little table that folded down from a cupboard in the wall. There was a clean linen towel and a flannel cloth too and a lump of yellow soap and a basin. Emma shrugged off her shawl and rolled up her sleeves and pulled her hair back. Outside, she could hear the old woman talking to the horse, and her voice sounded almost gentle. Emma poured hot water into the basin and cooled it with the cold. It would be a comfort to have a good wash in warm water, she thought.

As Emma scrubbed her face and neck, her forearms and her hands, she looked about her with delight. The tiny cabin was tidy and shining. Every inch of space, it seemed to her, was used for something—a drawer or a shelf or a cupboard. A bench ran along the wall opposite the stove, and a little painted stool stood near. Lace screened the small round windows and edged every shelf. There was even a ruffle across the ceiling toward the back of the cabin, with lace-edged curtains drawn aside beneath it. Every bit of woodwork was decorated with designs of painted flowers. There were gleaming horse brasses hanging on the walls and beautiful bits of crockery—plates and cups and a big brown teapot—sitting on a shelf, and a shiny brass lantern on a bracket. It looked as cozy as their cottage used to look when Mother was alive.

At the thought of the cottage, Emma had a sudden vision of Nancy, peering anxiously from the cottage door. She would be looking for Emma by now and beginning to fret.

It canna be helped, Emma told herself. I'll start home in the morn as soon as it be light.

Emma was washing her feet when Mrs. Minshull popped her head through the cabin doorway.

"What d'ye think ye be doin', Emma Deane?" she cried. "Shed yer togs, I say. Ye canna have a proper wash that way."

Emma stared at the old woman in bewilderment. It was but a few weeks past that Nancy had unstitched the woolen undergarments padded with newspapers into which she had sewn Emma at the start of the cold weather. Emma had washed all over then, though Nancy had said it was still too cold to hazard washing her hair.

But now Mrs. Minshull stepped down into the cabin and jerked at Emma's buttons, her hands rough and careless.

Emma clutched closed the neck of her bodice and cried out, "Leave off, leave off! I be fair clean enough!"

"Na clean enough fer *this* cabin, Emma Deane," Mrs. Minshull said, but she took her hands away and stepped back. "We be na dirty like them what come from the bank to hire out on the cut. Shed ev'ry stitch," she warned, "or it'll go hard wi' ye. Toss yer togs to me. They be fit but fer rags."

"What shall I wear then?" said Emma.

Mrs. Minshull burrowed in a drawer beneath the bench and pulled out something white.

"This," she said, "but na 'til ye be ev'ry bit clean, hair and all. I've no wish fer me spare nightdress to get lousy."

Being quite undressed was the oddest feeling, Emma thought. She did not know why she was doing as the old woman ordered, except that it seemed beyond imagining to do aught else.

As the water in the basin dirtied, Emma passed it up to Mrs. Minshull on deck to throw overboard. Then she would pour fresh water into the empty basin and scrub another part of herself, using the flannel cloth and the strong yellow soap. Her skin began to feel sore from the scrubbing, and her face was hot and perspiring.

She had to stand almost with her head in the basin while she poured the teakettle water over. Her scalp tingled from the soap, and she could feel how hopelessly knotted her tangles were as she combed her fingers through her wet hair. Three dead fleas floated on the water in the basin. Mrs. Minshull called to her that she would help, but Emma was ashamed to be seen without clothes.

When finally she pulled the white nightdress over her head, it seemed to Emma that she was inside someone else's skin, so strange did she feel. She saw that there was crocheted lace at the neck and the sleeves and the hem of the nightdress. It was pretty enough to wear to church, she thought.

But when Mrs. Minshull called to her to come out of the cabin, she felt shy.

"I have na me clothes," she said.

"There's naught about but ye and me," said the old woman, "and I've laid eyes in me time on lasses clad in less than a nightdress."

Emma was shocked, but she did as she was bidden.

When she emerged, dusk had fallen. She shivered in the breeze, cool after the heat of the cabin.

"Set yerself down," Mrs. Minshull said, brushing past her. She reappeared with the lit lantern and a comb.

The whole time that Mrs. Minshull was parting and combing through Emma's hair, she scolded—for the water spilled on the cabin floor, for the linen towel now stained and sopping, for the drowned fleas and lice she was unearthing with her fine-toothed comb.

"Ow!" cried Emma again and again, as the old woman yanked the comb through the snarls. But tender as her head was growing beneath the onslaught, Mrs. Minshull's fussing was oddly comforting.

Nancy will na know me, she thought. I'll be right comely wi' me hair combed neat and me face clean.

It was full dark, with the moths pattering against the lantern's chimney, when at last Mrs. Minshull had combed and plaited Emma's hair to her satisfaction. She was still muttering and threatening Emma with fleabane as she led the way down into the cabin and set out bread and cheese and ale for their tea. The bread was fresh and plentiful, the cheese strong, and the ale cool in Emma's parched mouth. She began to feel sleepy—not bone tired and sore as after a day in the mill, but heavy-limbed and fresh from her wash and sun-tender in her new skin.

It seemed like magic when Mrs. Minshull let down a bed from out of a cupboard behind the curtains at the back of the cabin. For Emma she unrolled a thin mattress and laid it on the bench.

"This be the side bed," she said, handing Emma a clean woolen blanket. "'Tis na fit fer a lass to sleep on a pallet in the hold as young Tom did."

The old woman climbed into the bed that had come out of the cupboard to fit in front of the little door to the hold. She drew the curtains before it.

"Sleep well, lass. There be sixteen locks at Marple. We mun make an early start."

Emma sank down on the bench—the "side bed," Mrs. Minshull had called it, as she had called her own the "cross bed."

"Ye say this river journeys to Manchester?" Emma said as she pulled up the scratchy blanket.

She could hear Mrs. Minshull stirring behind the curtains.

"Canal, lass. This be a canal, not a river," said the old woman. "We call it 'the cut,' fer God made rivers and streams, but men cut the canals."

Canal. Emma had heard folk speak of the canal and of the narrowboats that plied it, taking goods from place to place, but she had not realized it ran so close to home.

Just behind the wall, she thought. It be there all the time, and I na knowing.

It would be a fine thing to see the great city of Manchester. It was a shame that she must go home in the morn.

I mun tell the old woman I canna help her on the morrow, she thought, and she tried to say the words out loud. But her tongue seemed too heavy to move.

The boat floated gently on the still water with quiet, creaking sounds, and the mattress smelled sweet beneath her cheek.

I'll be up afore she wakes, Emma thought. I can go on me way without her interfering.

And then she was asleep.

# WORK

EMMA HAD BEEN PUT TO WORK IN THE MILL the year that she was seven, the year Mother and Father and brother Joe and the baby sister had died of the cholera. Their deaths had left only Emma and Nancy, who was fourteen.

Ben Jackson had seemed then like a hero to the bewildered and grief-stricken Emma. He was big and strong and full of plans, proud of his engineer's job.

"It be steady work and well paid," he had told Nancy when he offered marriage. "Wi' yer wages and her'n, we might soon buy the cottage," he had said.

So Nancy had agreed.

"One year's toil, and ye can sit at home like a lady," Ben had promised her. "The little un can go a scholar to the Chapel school."

It was a fine prospect . . . and what else were they going to do, but go to the poorhouse?

Emma remembered her first days in the mill. The close, impure air stifled her, and she was deafened by the clamor of the machines. She was so frightened that she could not speak a word, not even to Nancy, who was soon set to work winding and warping dyed silk in another part of the mill.

An older girl had been set to teach Emma how to fasten the silk ends together, but Emma's fingers had trembled violently.

"Here now," the girl had said. "Ye dinna want a floggin', do ye? A sucking babe could do this. Look sharp, I say!"

Emma had burst into tears.

She had been allowed to sit on a stool in the corner until she could stop crying. The kindly girl stood before the swifts and twisted her threads for her until Emma was able to try again. Finally, with great difficulty, Emma had found a loose thread in a whirling slip of silk. Somewhat more easily, she had also found the end of the silk on the bobbin below and had twisted them together. Shortly, she had six swifts to keep going, and the girl left her to herself.

"See now, ye'll do fine," she had said.

The next day, the steward met Emma at the door when she and Nancy arrived. He took Emma to a side of swifts and said, "Start here, girl, and let us see what thou canst do."

Again, Emma's fingers began to tremble, and she thought she would sink to the floor in despair.

"Humph!" said the steward. "Thou'rt not up to much."

Emma never forgot the hot flood of anger she had felt as he turned away. She remembered how she had stood there, stubbornly working out for herself that the broken threads could be found by watching for slowing bobbins. Her eyes searched the slips in the dim light for the loose, whirling threads, and little by little she had begun to find and twist them. When the steward returned, she had eight swifts going.

"Set her a dozen," the steward told the older girl.

The next day when he came by, Emma had the dozen swifts going.

"Hmm," said the steward. "Set her twenty."

A few weeks later, Emma had become aware one day of the steward standing behind her again.

"Thou'll do now, girl," he had said, and to the older girl, "Set her twenty-five."

Ben had said a year, but before the year was up, Nancy's first baby had come. There was the midwife's fee and the time when Nancy was too weak to work and the need of baby things. With no extra money for buying the cottage, they continued to lease it as Emma's folks had done. Emma kept on at the mill.

The second year, Ben broke his leg, and when he was well again, his job had gone to another. He found only half-day work. Then the baby died, and Nancy was taken ill. They began to sell their bits and pieces. Emma kept on at the mill.

The third year, Ben lost even his half-day's work. They sublet the loft and then the upper rooms. Nancy's second baby was born, and she refused to leave it. Ben took to drink. Emma kept on at the mill.

It had been her life—standing before the whirling swifts ten hours each day, her fingers flying among the threads, her thoughts wandering among the colors and patterns of the silk. There was only a break for dinner and twenty minutes baggin' time for tea and wheaten bread. The mill by day, then home exhausted to catch what uneasy sleep she could when Nancy and Ben weren't quarreling and the baby wasn't crying and the upstairs folk fell quiet.

On the boat that night, Emma slept as though rocked in a cradle, and when she opened her eyes the next morning, it was to the lantern's light. Mrs. Minshull was clattering at the stove beside her, and Emma could smell treacle and bread soaking in hot water, such as Nancy made for breakfast when they had the good fortune of treacle.

She raised herself on her elbow, her stomach suddenly griping with hunger—and I had such a tea last eve as I shouldn't want food fer a fortnight! she thought in wonder.

Then she remembered that she'd meant to be up and gone before Mrs. Minshull awakened.

"Good mornin', lass," said the old woman, gesturing to a pile of garments stacked at Emma's feet. "Ye mun wear those," she said. "I can see we'll have to visit the bootmaker when we get to Manchester, fer yer feet'll na stand many more days o' walkin' barefoot."

Boots? thought Emma, her breath catching in her throat. The thought so dazed her that she did not remember until later that Mrs. Minshull had said "many more days."

Emma found herself sitting on the edge of the bench, pulling cotton drawers up under her nightdress, then a shift and stuff gown down over her head. They must belong to Mrs. Minshull, she thought, but they were none too big for Emma, the old woman was so small. They were stiff and clean, as Emma imagined new clothes must be, and Emma wondered as she tied on the long fawn-colored apron, was the old woman *giving* them to her?

Mrs. Minshull was already dressed in similar garb, and she wore the black poke bonnet on her head. Emma noticed the sturdy boots on her feet. Had she said she would buy boots for Emma?

Emma's last boots had come from the pawnbroker two autumns agone, and had never fit properly. First they were too big and then, over the last winter, Emma's feet had grown so that she had ceased wearing them as soon as the frost was gone. Cold was preferable to rubbed-raw toes.

Her head swimming with thoughts of boots and her body feeling strange in unfamiliar clothes and her belly full of warm sop, Emma soon found herself on the bank without protest, helping harness Rosie in the dim light of dawn.

Rosie's pale coat seemed to glow, Emma could see by

the lightening sky. Mrs. Minshull must have brushed her last evening while Emma was washing. The white flounces of hair around her great feet were clean of burrs and dust, and her mane and tail were as smooth as Emma's fresh braids.

"Ye shall have proper stablin' this night, me luv," Mrs. Minshull was murmuring as she fastened various buckles. Emma heard that same tender tone she had heard in the old woman's voice last night. It was not a tone she had used to Emma.

"Give her an extra measure o' oats," she barked, handing Rosie's nose tin to Emma. "She deserves a good breakfast after standin' out i' the damp all night."

Where did Rosie usually spend the night, Emma wondered as she filled the tin from the sack of oats Mrs. Minshull had indicated. But she did not ask. It was impossible to ask questions of the old woman, her ways were so confounding. It did not really signify, Emma thought, for by evening she, Emma, would have to be safely home.

Yet she did not turn toward home when at last they had the boat afloat. Who, after all, she told herself, would drive Rosie if she abandoned Mrs. Minshull? She thought of the promised boots. Perhaps she owed her a few more hours for all her gruff intended kindness.

The walking was easier today, Emma thought as she listened to the thud of Rosie's hooves ahead of her. Though Emma had been stiff in every muscle when she woke, the stiffness eased as the sun rose. It would be another clear blue day, she saw, and she settled her pace to match Rosie's, closing her mind to thoughts of home and taking comfort in the more and more familiar feeling of the path beneath her feet.

Before long, around a bend, she saw cottages clustered near the canal's edge. A boy was herding sheep from a pen, and a woman threw slops from her door.

Then ahead, just beyond three close-set bridges, the canal widened, then narrowed, and Emma saw that a white-painted barrier blocked the channel. As they approached it, the boat headed toward the bank. When the boat bumped against the canal side, Rosie obligingly stopped. In an instant, Mrs. Minshull hopped to land and was tying the boat to rings, hidden in the grass.

"Rosie'll stand," Mrs. Minshull said as she hurried past Emma toward the barrier. "*She* knows what to do. Come along, and I'll show ye the locks."

Locks. Emma remembered the old woman had said something about locks when she was telling Emma what she must do to work off her debt. Were there locks on the barrier that Emma must open?

"Come along, I say," came Mrs. Minshull's impatient voice.

Emma jerked to follow.

Beyond the barrier, Emma found herself looking into a narrow pond edged with brickwork. There were wooden doors at each end, holding in the water.

"This here be yer windlass," Mrs. Minshull was saying, and Emma found a bent brass rod shoved into her hands. "Dinna mislay it," Mrs. Minshull snapped. Emma saw that the old woman had another, thrust into a wide leather belt at her waist.

Mrs. Minshull cupped her hand to her mouth and hollered, "Hallo, Jock Nevins, be ye about? I've no time to waste awaitin' on ye!"

But no one answered.

"Curse the man for the wastrel he be!" Mrs. Minshull muttered. "We can work as well wi'out him. The lock be set. Just help me wi' this gate."

# CYGNET'S HUFFLER

MRS. MINSHULL LEANED HER BACK against a great blunt wooden beam that reached across from the top of the barrier door and overhung the path beside it. She heaved backward, and Emma watched in amazement as the barrier began to swing open. Emma put her own backside against the beam and helped Mrs. Minshull push until the gate, as Mrs. Minshull called it, stood open.

"When I be ready," Mrs. Minshull said, "ye can lead our Rosie up, then close the gate behind me."

In only a moment, it seemed to Emma, the old woman stood in the stern of the boat, gesturing to her.

Rosie seemed to be dreaming, her head between her legs, but she roused when she felt Emma's hand on her harness and leaned into her collar. The boat glided into the narrow pond and bumped against the front doors.

Emma would not have thought the boat would fit, so close was the space, but it did, with only a hand span or so to spare all around. Emma and Rosie stopped.

Then . . . confusion! Bewildering shouted commands from the old woman to close the gate, then to wind the paddles, to do Emma knew not what. She found herself straining at the wooden beam that closed the gate and heaving with her windlass at an iron mechanism on the doors at the far end of the pond.

Below the doors, Emma saw that the land fell steeply away. With a catch of her breath, she saw that the canal continued below, as though at the bottom of a cliff.

"Cross over!" Mrs. Minshull was barking.

There was a plank footbridge fastened to the doors, hanging over the steep drop.

Cross that rickety bridge?

Emma looked at the old woman beseechingly, but Mrs. Minshull only glared.

There was no handrail on the footbridge, and Emma's legs began to tremble as she imagined plunging from it into the cut below, but Mrs. Minshull was shrieking and gesturing. Emma, accustomed to obedience for fear of a caning from a foreman or a lamming from Ben, took a deep breath and forced her foot onto the bridge.

"Cross over and wind up the other paddle," Mrs. Minshull cried impatiently.

Emma put her other foot upon the bridge and, trying not to look down, stepped shakily across, her temples pounding and her breath coming fast. She almost sank down when she felt solid ground beneath her.

"Wind up, wind up!" yelled Mrs. Minshull from the boat.

Emma looked in bewilderment at her and was astonished to see that the boat was beginning to sink slowly below the edge of the pond. The water was leaking out, she saw, on the other side from which she had come, and as it lowered, the boat went down. Dumfounded, Emma stared openmouthed until Mrs. Minshull shouted at her again. The old woman wanted her to crank the mechanism on this side of the pond as she had done on the other side, and she suddenly understood. That would lift the paddles, as Mrs. Minshull called them, some unseen device that let the water out. She leaned hard, throwing her whole weight against it, to make the windlass turn. Sweat sprang out beneath her arms. The smell of grease and metal was strong in her nose. It was the smell of machinery, Emma thought, the smell of the mill, and she hated it. I'll na stay another hour if this be the work she'd have me do, she vowed to herself. I'll . . .

"Hallo, *Cygnet!*" boomed a voice beneath her, making Emma jump just as she was giving a final turn to her windlass. She saw a man in brown corduroys climbing the steep stone steps that led up the hill beside the wooden doors.

"*Cygnet?*" said Emma, panting. She remembered she had heard the word before.

"Aye, ain't that the name o' yer boat, missy? Ain't that old Granny Minshull's *Cygnet* yon? Where be that scalawag Tom?"

"Buggered off," replied Emma, half distracted. Once again, she was watching in astonishment as the boat sank even more quickly toward the level of the lower canal. Water was gushing out into the canal beneath the doors and rushing downstream toward a bridge. This was what they had been doing, she understood suddenly. They were lowering the boat downhill!

"So yer *Cygnet*'s huffler now?" said the man.

Emma turned toward him, blinking with wonder at what she and Mrs. Minshull had just done. For a long moment, she considered the question, and then she nodded.

"Aye," Emma said.

"I see ye've torn yerself from bed, Jock Nevins!" Mrs. Minshull was crying from deep in the dripping brick hole. "I thought the Company'd sacked ye fer playin' Tom Noddie."

"Ye be as sweet-tempered as e'er, Granny," replied the man, laughing.

"I be half a day late, and a green lass fer a huffler, that's what I be," shouted Mrs. Minshull.

"A right willin' lass too, I'll be bound," said Jock Nevins, winking at Emma. "She just needs a bit o' schoolin'. Jock Nevins'll take ye down, missy, ne'er ye fear. I be the best lock keeper in England. When ye've done the Marples wi' Jock Nevins, there be nothin' ye won't know 'bout locks."

Emma could hear Mrs. Minshull snort. But the man spoke so kindly, and his crinkly brown face was so good-natured, that she ventured a question.

"Where *be* these locks yer on about?" she said.

"Why, *this* be a lock, missy. This what yer boat sits in. A lock be fer carryin' boats uphill or down."

"I be gloppened!" said Emma. "I thought she meant a lock wi' a key."

Jock Nevins threw back his head and laughed.

"Ye *do* be green, missy," he said. "We'd best commence yer schoolin' straightaway."

With Jock's help and gentle instructions, it was an easy matter to let the boat out of the emptied lock. As she drove Rosie down the steep path from the lock, Emma heaved a sigh. She was glad to have that done with.

Jock sprinted down from the closed doors, where he had let the last paddles down, and walked beside her.

"Where did Granny Minshull come across *ye*, missy?" he asked.

But Emma was suddenly loathe to tell him how she came to be with the old woman, lest it reflect unkindly on her.

"Macclesfield," she said shortly, and then, beyond a stone bridge, she caught sight of the beams of another white-painted barrier gate.

"Be that *another* lock?" she asked Jock Nevins, gesturing, and once again he threw back his head to laugh.

"Aye, missy, so it be, and another beyond, and another beyond that."

Suddenly Emma remembered Mrs. Minshull's words from the night before. "There be sixteen locks at Marple," she had said.

Emma stopped still in the path.

"Sixteen!" she cried, dismayed.

"Aye, sixteen," said Jock Nevins proudly. "The finest locks on the cut!"

Emma nodded weakly, pondering this information, and Jock Nevins began to tell her about locks and the fittest way to shift them.

There was no further time to think that morning. The locks came fast upon one another, and each seemed slightly different to Emma, though they all had in common the opening and closing of gates, the winding up and down of the paddles that let the water out. Once Mrs. Minshull came ashore and showed Emma how to check Rosie's hooves for pebbles and her harness for chafing. She told Emma to take off the nose tin, so that Rosie could graze when the boat was in a lock, and reminded Emma to water her often.

Several times they passed other boats working upward, and Jock taught her that the rope of an unladen boat always passed over the boat with a load. He showed her the latch on the cabin chimney that allowed Mrs. Minshull to tilt it before the oncoming rope. There were other boats behind and before them, he said, as well as the boats they passed, and some towed a second boat, which Jock Nevins called a "butty."

"The cut be a lively road," he said.

He seems to know everything, Emma thought, her head spinning with all she was learning. He knew every*one* as well, for he greeted them all by name. Time and again, he left the *Cygnet* for a while to help some other boat.

Emma saw other women steering. They wore flounced bonnets as Mrs. Minshull did, and sometimes their little children were harnessed to the chimneys on the flat cabin roofs—so they would not fall into the water, Emma guessed. Once Emma saw a girl her own age driving a horse, but mostly it was boys or men.

The locks were like stairs for boats, Emma thought. It did not surprise her to hear Jock Nevins call the sixteen locks together a "flight," for that was what stairs were called as well.

Emma's hands grew sore from turning her windlass, and she knew she would have blisters. The sun beat hotter and hotter as it climbed in the sky, and Emma longed for a bonnet to protect her face and neck. But despite these discomforts, she thought no more of leaving the boat, so taken up by the work was she. A wind sprang up, and she could hear Mrs. Minshull cursing as it blew the boat sideways when she tried to enter a lock. Jock Nevins laughed.

After the fifth lock, Emma lost count and so was surprised when she heard Jock Nevins say, "Well and away, missy. Ye be a proper lockman now, and no mistake. Dinna leave the old woman mither ye. She be a good old soul at heart. I'll be lookin' fer ye the next time ye come through."

She looked ahead and realized there were no more barrier gates in sight. This time, Jock did not follow her but stood, his hand uplifted, beside the last lock.

"Fare thee well, missy," he cried. "Fare thee well, Granny."

Emma was astonished to hear Mrs. Minshull calling back, "Bless ye, Jock Nevins. We be through in good time!"

# FLOWERS
## *in the* DUST

EMMA WISHED THE OLD WOMAN would bring the boat to the bank to rest awhile. Though she was elated with all she had learned and done at the locks, she was also exhausted. Her breath came in gasps, and her sweat-damp clothes clung to her skin. Her hands and shoulders ached.

They passed beneath three bridges, one of them for trains, and crossed high over a river on what Emma had been naming to herself a "water bridge," but which Jock Nevins had called an "aqueduct." When Mrs. Minshull disappeared into the cabin for a moment and reappeared with a handkerchief-wrapped bundle, Emma realized they were apt to keep on until night or Manchester, whichever happened first.

She stumbled on a tree root but was glad of the tree's shade. Rosie, she saw, was not tired. She had had plenty of rest, waiting by the locks. She was not hungry either,

Emma thought. Not hungry as Emma was hungry, with a weakness that spread from her empty belly to her heavy, aching limbs. She wondered why Mrs. Minshull did not call to her to fetch her dinner from the extended pike. Again and again, Emma looked back at the boat, where her dinner sat on the cabin roof beside the pikes and the mop and the painted water cans. But Mrs. Minshull did not call. She seemed to have forgotten Emma's dinner. Indeed, she seemed to have forgotten Emma, for her eyes were fixed on the canal ahead, and her hand on the tiller pushed it this way and that as the cut wound past a wooded hillside.

"I'd liefer be her horse than her huffler, Rosie," Emma said, walking abreast of the horse, "for she rests and feeds and waters *thee*."

Rosie snorted and tossed her head, setting the tassels on her cap dancing.

"Ye've e'en got a bonnet," Emma said, gingerly wiping the sweat from her stinging neck, "and shoes fer yer feet!" She wondered again whether Mrs. Minshull truly meant to buy boots for her. Emma's toe was sore where she had stubbed it, and a bruise on her heel made her limp. Each painful step was taking her farther and farther from all she had ever known. Once again, she began to smart at the way the old woman had cozened her.

Indeed, so sunk was she in cataloging her grievances that it was some moments before she realized that Mrs. Minshull was now calling.

She looked back and saw that the boat had edged

close to the towpath. Dinner, she wondered, but Mrs. Minshull was pointing ahead. Emma looked where she pointed and saw a black hole opening in the hillside. The canal flowed into it. She cupped a hand to her ear.

"Tunnel!" Mrs. Minshull was yelling, as though Emma could not see for herself. "Ye can sup when ye've taken Rosie 'round."

Emma had no notion what the old woman was on about. Take Rosie 'round where?

She could see that, ahead, a pair of boats was moored at the canal's edge. Their horse was nowhere in sight, but a boatman was striding toward Emma on the path. *Cygnet* slid along the bank, and Mrs. Minshull threw a rope to the man. He looped it around a bollard on the bank and tugged the boat to a stop just clear of his butty.

I could have done that, Emma thought. She could have tossed the rope to *me*, for Jock Nevins showed me how to stop the boat. She does na trust me, though Jock said I were right handy!

Rosie had stopped. She was snuffling about in the bottom of her nose tin, and Emma could tell it was empty. She unfastened it from the bridle, and Rosie blew her warm breath against Emma's hands. As aggrieved as she felt, Emma smiled and rubbed the horse's nose, wondering how she could have feared the gentle creature.

"*Ye* be me friend, Rosie," she whispered.

Mrs. Minshull brought Emma's handkerchief-wrapped dinner ashore.

"The boat mun be legged through," she said. "There

be a boat afore us and one comin' through now, so 'twill
be a time. Ye can take Rosie 'round yon hill''—she ges-
tured to the towpath, which wound up and away from
the cut—"and wait fer us at t'other end." She looked at
Emma's feet and frowned. "The bootmaker'll not come
too soon," she said. "Rest yer pore feets while ye wait."

Emma felt ashamed of her hard thoughts. The dinner
bundle was heavy in her hand, and a good smell came
from it. The old woman seemed worried about her sore
feet. She had told her to rest.

"Thank ye kindly," Emma said.

But Mrs. Minshull only said, "Get along wi' ye!" and
waved her away.

Emma hurried to unhitch Rosie before Mrs.
Minshull could help. I can do it meself, she thought.

As she led the horse along the path, she saw another
horse coming down from the hill and, a few moments
later, a boat nosing its way out of the tunnel. A plank had
been rigged to each side of the boat's bow, and on each
plank lay a man on his back, moving the boat along by
walking his feet, leg over leg, against the tunnel walls.
That must be what Mrs. Minshull meant by "legged
through," she thought.

It was odd not to have the canal flowing beside the
path as they climbed the steeply sloping hill. Emma saw
cows grazing nearby and felt uneasy that there was no
hedge between her and them. Up close, cows seemed to
her big and clumsy-footed, with something wild in their
eyes. She kept as far as she could from the ones who

munched the grass near the path. But the cows paid her no mind.

Rosie, after all, was even bigger than the cows, she told herself. And she was not afraid of Rosie.

On the other side of the hill, Emma saw that the path rejoined the canal just at the tunnel's mouth. There were no boats or men in sight, but a horse was tethered beside the path. Emma knew that its driver must be near, so instead of leading Rosie to the water, she stopped beside a large flat stone halfway down the hill. She tied Rosie to a sapling and sat on the stone to eat.

Emma opened the handkerchief and found, as she had the day before, a bottle of tea. Today there was also a chunk of rye bread, which Mrs. Minshull had purchased from a lock-side cottage, and cheese and an apple.

"She don't stint on the grub," Emma told Rosie. "I'll say that in her favor." Then her mouth was too full to speak.

When the last crumb was eaten, Emma shook out the handkerchief and wrapped it about the empty bottle. She gave Rosie the apple core on the flat of her hand as Mrs. Minshull had showed her and giggled at the whiskery tickle of Rosie's lips on her palm.

The boat that had been waiting on the other side emerged with its butty from the tunnel. Emma saw a boy rise from the tall grass of the verge to hitch up the waiting horse.

He must have been resting, sleeping mayhap, in the grass, Emma thought.

She watched carefully to see how the hitching was accomplished, how the planks were stowed and the leggers paid off by the boatman. The boatman's wife came out to sit on the cabin roof, a baby in her arms. Emma could hear its lusty crying, and she thought of Nancy's baby and the weak mewling sound it made. It was hard, sitting here in the clear air of the country, to imagine Nancy's baby. Smoky Macclesfield seemed distant and far in the past. It seemed a different life.

How'll Nancy manage without me wages, Emma wondered. Would she have to leave her baby with Mrs. Mullins next door and take Emma's place in the mill?

Emma's heart sank to think of it. When Nancy's first baby died in Mrs. Mullins's care, Nancy had vowed never to leave a nursing child of hers again. "Nay, though I go to the poorhouse!" she had said. It was dosing the baby to keep it from crying had killed it, Nancy said. "Why shouldn't the poor mite cry when it be hungry?" she had sobbed. "It cried for its mam, and I were na there!"

The leggers were tramping past Emma's rock. The younger lifted his cap. "We'll be na long," he said pleasantly, and Emma nodded, not meeting his eyes.

Perhaps Ben would find a job, she thought. He was always saying that something would turn up. He was a good hand with engines, Ben said, and if the owners had any sense, they'd not let a good man go to waste. Except that he'd been going to waste this twelvemonth, and the job before that had lasted scarce a fortnight. There were many good men without work in these hard times, and many good wives who toiled in the mills with no time or strength for their babies. Emma thought the loss of that first baby was what had sent Ben to drink, and when this babe was born, he'd have naught to do with it. He would not even look at it at first. "Ye be a fool to mither wi' it," he had told Nancy. "Ye'll only break yer heart." But Nancy didn't listen. She set her mouth and made do on Emma's wages and was gentle with the baby and with Ben too. "This child'll na die," she told him, as though her telling made it so.

The leggers had disappeared over the crest of the hill, and Emma knew that she should take Rosie to the cut to be ready when the boat came through. But instead, she lay facedown on the rock and let the sun soak into her. She felt suddenly dispirited. What be I doing here, she thought, when I be needed home?

The fingers of one hand trailed in the dust, and Emma watched them as though they did not belong to her, emptying her mind of all else. She leaned her face over the edge of the stone and watched the lines her fingers scratched, watched the way the dust swirled in patterns. It eddied softly about her fingertips, and a tear splashed into the pattern, leaving a dark shape at its center. She stared at the shape until it seemed to her to resemble a flower, and then she began to trace other flowers around it, like the flowers painted on Mrs. Minshull's boat. With a twig she added details. With a blade of grass she softened the edges of the petals. She did not allow herself to think again until Mrs. Minshull called.

The old woman was vexed.

"Ye be as feckless as that lad Tom!" she cried. "We mun get the boat ahead, lass. That be the thing wi' haulin'. We mun get the boat ahead!"

For the rest of the way, Emma jumped quickly to do Mrs. Minshull's bidding. She trudged silently behind Rosie, scarcely noticing how the cottages and mills grew closer together as they neared the city. She did not respond when passing folk greeted her. The sun no longer comforted, but burned and made her sweat. Flies buzzed her hanging head. Her feet pained. Her throat felt parched, but she did not ask for drink.

Emma formed and re-formed in her mind the pictures she had made in the dust. As she used to do standing before her swifts in the mill, she imagined colors that her eyes did not see. She envisioned shapes and lines and curves. She invented patterns of garlands and nosegays.

She did not allow herself to think of home.

# MANCHESTER

MANCHESTER WAS SO LIKE MACCLESFIELD that Emma wondered why she had longed to see it. There were the same soot-stained buildings, rising so close together and near the canal that the sun was blotted out. There was the same thick, foul-smelling air, the same dark smoke rising from chimneys, the same mired and noisome streets.

They tied up at an oily, splintered dock beside a hulking warehouse, and Mrs. Minshull pointed a gnarled finger at the building next to it where an inn sign creaked in the breeze.

"There be stables yon," she said. "See to th'animal. The boy'll show ye how. Then haste back to help wi' th'unloadin'."

Emma nodded dully and set off with Rosie for the inn stables. Rosie seemed to know the way. In her eagerness, she almost brushed Emma off the dock as she shouldered past her.

The stable boy recognized Rosie, but he gave Emma a dark, mistrustful look.

"Where be Tom then?" he wanted to know. "Where be th'old woman?"

Emma returned his scowl.

"Tom's buggered off. Mrs. Minshull be seein' to th'unloadin', and *I* be her huffler now."

But she could not maintain her bravado for long.

"Ye be not much of a hand wi' horses," the boy observed as he watched her struggle with Rosie's harness.

"I can learn," Emma muttered.

"Aye, mayhappen," said the boy, and Emma realized that he was helping.

When at last Rosie had been groomed, with the brushes that Emma had had to run back to fetch from the boat—she could have *told* me to take them, Emma thought—and was fed and stalled for the night, Emma did not feel so harshly toward the stable boy. He had indeed showed her how to brush Rosie's coat until it shone, standing on a stool to reach her high back and shoulders, and how to comb out her mane and tail and her great feathered feet. He had checked Rosie's shoes for stones and cleaned them, holding her hooves across his bent knee.

I could do that, thought Emma.

"She be a right trusty old horse, be Rosie," said the boy, and Emma flushed with pride.

"Aye, that she be," she said.

Emma would have liked to sink down on the clean straw of Rosie's stall and go straight to sleep, so weary was she. But the boy was dealing with another horse now, whose owner had hurried away after flipping him a coin.

"We mun unload afore dark," he had said, and that reminded Emma of Mrs. Minshull's orders.

"Well, an' ye were long enough at it," was all Mrs. Minshull said when Emma reappeared on the wharf.

The old woman was standing in the hold, the tarpaulins—or "top sheets," as she called them—thrown back to reveal the cargo, helping a red-haired man who was heaving sacks of potatoes over the side to the dock. Two burly men carried the sacks to the warehouse. Emma heard their groans as they hefted the sacks to their shoulders.

Emma climbed down into the boat and took hold of a sack. She could not lift it.

"Dinna hoist wi' yer back," the old woman grunted.

She seized the other side of the sack, and together they flung it over.

"Use yer legs," Mrs. Minshull instructed again and again. "Ne'er yer back, but yer legs."

But it seemed to Emma that it was her arms she was using to heave the sacks. Their ache became so steady that she thought she could not raise them. Her hands, used to the fine work of twisting silk, were soon scraped raw, the new blisters burst. Yet again and again she and Mrs. Minshull and the red-haired man hoisted the sacks from the boat.

How could so old and small a woman lift so much weight, Emma wondered.

The sweat poured off Emma until her bodice was soaked. Her breath seared her chest. After a while she moved through the pain mechanically, stooping and lifting and heaving without sight or thought.

When at last her reaching hands met no sack, she was too exhausted to feel glad. She sank down on the plank floor of the hold and fell over, sound asleep.

She woke on the side bed, tucked beneath the blanket and wearing the white nightdress. Vaguely, she remembered being lifted and carried here—was it the red-haired man who had carried her or tiny Mrs. Minshull herself? She remembered slumping against the cabin wall, half conscious, while her face and arms and hands were bathed with warm water and she was given something to drink.

Now, as she rolled, moaning, onto one elbow, the sun was shining through the open hatch, and a pot bubbled merrily on the stove beside her, its steam perfuming the air with a heady meaty smell. A growling voice was speaking from the deck above.

"Sell up, Aggie! Dinna be a fool! The Company'll give ye a fair price."

Emma had to strain to hear the reply, so quietly did Mrs. Minshull speak.

"Na while there be breath in me body, Jeb Hawkins."

"But, Aggie!" The growl rose louder. "Ye be right hobbled from unloadin' yesterday. Ye canna get a narrowboat ahead wi'out a man to help ye."

"I can, and I do."

"Ye were half a day late wi' those taters."

"Rosie threw a shoe. The boy run off. Me new huffler be green."

"Green? She looked half dead to me."

"She ne'er did flinch at th'unloadin'. She only needs feedin' up."

Emma pulled herself upright, aching in every bone. That was her they were talking about, Mrs. Minshull and the man with the growling voice. She cocked her head.

"She needs sendin' back to her mam," said the man.

There was a silence. Then Mrs. Minshull's voice rang firm.

"*He* ne'er would sell, nor will I. That be an end to it!"

"Ye be a mulish old woman, Ag Minshull."

"Aye, that I be."

"Next time they may na offer so good a price."

Emma could feel the boat sway. The growling man must have stepped off, she thought. She swung her legs over the side of the bed, wincing with pain.

"She ne'er did flinch," Mrs. Minshull had said of her.

And I dinna, she thought.

Shakily, Emma got to her feet and began to pull on her clothes.

"Wash!" barked Mrs. Minshull, appearing in the doorway. She handed down the washbasin to Emma. "Ye be sweated worse than Rosie," she said. "Ye'll find water in the kettle. And be quick about it. The bootmaker'll na wait on ye."

The bootmaker!

Whatever was cooking in the pot must have been for dinner and not for Emma's breakfast. When she was washed and dressed—I ne'er did see such a woman fer washin', she thought—Mrs. Minshull gave her a slab of wheaten bread and treacle to eat as she walked, and they climbed out of the cabin. Emma saw that the old woman moved slowly, as stooped and shaky as Emma felt— "hobbled," the growling voice had said.

The boat was no longer docked at the warehouse wharf, Emma saw when she emerged. They were tied alongside several other boats in a sort of inlet nearby. Two stout women washed laundry in tubs on the bank. Children played in an empty hold. She and Mrs. Minshull clambered stiffly from *Cygnet*'s deck to the next boat and then to the next and so to the bank.

"Beggin' yer pardon," Mrs. Minshull said politely to the people whose boats they crossed. The boat people greeted her. Emma thought they stared, but no one asked about her, and Mrs. Minshull did not name her to them.

They set out along a cobbled street leading away from the canal. Along it, the houses were close-set and mean, crowded in rows in the shadow of mills and warehouses. Some, Emma saw, were weavers' cottages like the one she and Nancy lived in, with their large-windowed garrets looking down on the street. Emma's father had once had his looms in their garret, and Emma's mother her spinning wheel. Emma remembered playing with the bright scraps of thread that littered the garret floor while the batten of Father's loom thumped above her head. But now the upstairs rooms and the garret were let to other families, and Nancy and Ben and Emma occupied only the ground-floor kitchen and scullery and slept by the hearth.

Emma tried to push away these nagging thoughts of home. She followed along beside the bent figure of Mrs. Minshull. Her own muscles were loosening and stretching as she walked, but the old woman still limped.

New boots! Emma told herself, wondering if the boots would be truly new or only new to her. Mrs. Minshull did say "bootmaker," Emma thought. She didn't say "pawnshop."

They turned a corner, and Emma saw that they had come out on a street of shops. There was the familiar pawnbroker's sign above one of them, and Emma's heart sank. But there was also a chandler—Emma could tell by the candles in the window—and a dry goods shop. . . . Mrs. Minshull disappeared suddenly through a low doorway. Emma followed and found herself breathing the clean, rich smell of leather and oil. As her eyes adjusted to the dimness, she saw shelves of shoes and boots and, sitting on a cobbler's bench, an old man with a pair of spectacles perched on his nose. He was tapping with a little hammer at something on his knee—wooden pegs into the shiny new sole of a boot.

# Boots and Bonnet

"Good day to ye, Mr. Collins," said Mrs. Minshull.

The old man on the cobbler's bench looked up, and his wrinkled face wrinkled still further in a grin.

"Mrs. Minshull," he said, "ye surely don't be needin' new boots. 'Twas but a year ago Whitsuntide ye had the last."

"Nay, na fer me, Mr. Collins, but fer me lass here. I canna have a barefoot huffler."

Emma, hanging back by the door, caught her breath. Mrs. Minshull had said "me lass" as though Emma belonged to her.

"Indeed, indeed." The little man was coming from his bench to peer at Emma over his spectacles. He dusted his hands together. "Sit ye down, sit ye down," he said, indicating a wooden stool to Emma and a chair to Mrs. Minshull. "She be right small and nesh," he said.

"Oh, she be small," said Mrs. Minshull, "but she be na nesh. Two days agone, she'd ne'er seen the cut. Yet though the journey were dree, she be na one o' them what's up on the roof or down the well, but steady an' willin'. And," she added, "Rosie takes to her."

"Ah, then," Mr. Collins said, kneeling and taking Emma's bare, dirty foot in his warm hands, "if Rosie takes to her, I'll reckon she'll do."

They waited three days in Manchester, though Mrs. Minshull insisted they waited for a cargo, as well as for Emma's boots.

Emma slept and slept. She could not remember ever sleeping so much. She was in bed of an evening shortly after dark, though Mrs. Minshull sat on the cross bed, sewing by lantern's light. Emma could hear the voices of the other boat people sitting on their cabin roofs. She could smell the scent of pipe smoke wafting across the water. There was the smell of cooking too and sometimes the sound of singing from the nearby inn. Listening, Emma fell swiftly to sleep and slept all night.

When she woke there was the boat to clean—the paintwork to mop and rinse with thrown buckets of canal water, the hold to sweep and scrub, the rope work to scour until it was white. She and Mrs. Minshull turned out the cabin, though to Emma it had seemed already spotless. The stove was emptied of ashes and blacked. The shelves and drawers were dusted. The brass ornaments were polished until they shone. The laundry was washed in tubs on the bank and hung in the empty hold to dry. The mattresses were shaken and the bedding aired. Mrs. Minshull folded away Tom's sleeping pallet. That be the end o' Tom, Emma thought.

Sometimes, even with all the work, there was time for a nap after dinner.

And such dinners! Mrs. Minshull simmered savory stews in the pot before the fire or soups thick with barley and potherbs. Each day she sent Emma to the bakery for a crusty loaf of bread. She traded a length of crocheted lace for a peck of last autumn's apples.

Emma liked to hear the easy way the boat people talked. Usually, when a new boat arrived at the moorage, it was greeted with hearty "How do's." When a boat departed, there were no farewells but only "See yer again." Just once, when the arriving boat was ill-kept—its horse lamed, its captain dirty and unshaved—did the others greet it with silence. "'Tis one o' them Company hirelin's," Mrs. Minshull muttered. "They got no pride, them hirelin's. They be too soon come from the bank."

Most of the Number Ones, the boatmen who owned their own boats, seemed to know one another. Everyone knew Mrs. Minshull. It was from their talk that Emma began to realize that there had been a *Mister* Minshull, who had died not long since.

"I be that sorry to hear o' the mister's passin'," one woman said.

"He were a pow'rful fine boatman, Mr. Minshull," said another.

"I shall miss him," a swarthy man said.

To all, Mrs. Minshull offered a simple "thank ye." But if anyone suggested that now she would retire, her lips tightened and her face grew stiff. "I do well enough," she would say, and once, Emma was dismayed to hear, "There be the lass to crew me."

What will she do when I go home, Emma wondered.

On the last day in Manchester, once again Mrs. Minshull set out along the cobbled street to the boot-maker's shop, and Emma followed.

In the dim shop, Mrs. Minshull drew from her pocket a pair of knitted stockings and bade Emma put them on. Then Mr. Collins himself eased Emma's feet into a pair of sturdy black hobnailed boots and laced them up.

"Walk about a bit," he commanded, and Emma did so, testing the unfamiliar feel of the boots on her feet, luxuriating in their warmth and shine, noting how she seemed to walk a little above the floor, unable to feel the texture of the splintery planks—or the sharpness of stones on the towpath, she thought, or the cold wet of muck.

"Aye, they fit well enough," said Mr. Collins, pressing on the hard toes. "They dinna rub at the heels?"

Emma shook her head, too overcome to speak.

"They dinna creak," said Mrs. Minshull in a satisfied voice.

Mr. Collins drew himself up. "Me boots ne'er do creak," he said, "and well ye know it, Mrs. Minshull."

Emma was surprised to see the smile in Mrs. Minshull's eyes.

"That I do, Mr. Collins," she said, reaching into her pocket for her purse.

Emma was shocked to see how many coins Mrs. Minshull counted into the boot maker's hand. How long mun I work to pay it back, she wondered.

But fretted as she was by the cost of the boots, Emma could not help but take joy in them as they walked back to the boat. She thought that everyone must see that she, Emma Deane, was wearing boots made particularly for her—the first new articles of clothing she could remember wearing. Carefully she stepped around puddles and horse plops. She scarcely lifted her eyes from her shiny toes, for it seemed to her they might disappear should she look away.

"Watch where yer goin'," Mrs. Minshull barked. "Ye'll walk straight into the cut, if ye dinna pay heed."

Emma raised her eyes to the old woman's face. Mrs. Minshull's beady gaze was fixed on her without expression.

"Oh, Mrs. Minshull," Emma said, catching at her arm. "Oh, Mrs. Minshull, I thank ye. I thank ye kindly!"

Mrs. Minshull sniffed.

"'Tis but boots," she said.

It was on that last afternoon that Mrs. Minshull took from the soap hole, the little cupboard where she kept her rags and brushes and soap, some small pots of colored paint and a long-handled brush.

"Me roses needs touchin' up," she said, and Emma watched, fascinated, as the old woman began to stroke fresh paint on the flower patterns of the cabin doors. Emma watched how Mrs. Minshull held the brush, something like the way Emma had been taught to hold her slate pencil. She saw the way the soft bristles swept on the color, fresh and shining.

I'd fancy doing that, Emma thought, but she said nothing, only watched.

"*He* were right particular 'bout his paintwork," Mrs. Minshull said. "We'll ne'er let down now *he's* gone."

Emma realized that Mrs. Minshull had included her in that "we."

On the day they left the moorage, Emma rose at dawn with Mrs. Minshull and helped her to stow the cross bed and mattresses in their cupboard. They washed in cold water and ate a hurried breakfast of bread and lard before crawling out of the warm cabin into the cool, gray morning.

"It be a shame to take on coal, and us so tidylike," Mrs. Minshull sighed, "but 'tis th'only cargo I could find. Step lively now o'er to the stable and fetch Rosie. They be awaitin' on us at the coal yard."

Emma thought that Rosie was glad to see her. The horse whinnied a greeting and nuzzled her with her soft nose.

"I have na apple fer ye today." Emma stroked the horse between her eyes before she began putting on the harness. She had come every evening with Mrs. Minshull to walk the horse around the stable yard and to give her a treat. "Yer holiday be o'er, old girl," she said, and it occurred to Emma that her own holiday was over as well.

The coal yard men shoveled the coal into *Cygnet's* hold. Mrs. Minshull made sure the coal was evenly distributed and leveled it with a rake. Emma was bidden to take Rosie to a nearby grassy place to graze.

By midmorning the boat was loaded and Rosie had once again been hitched to the mast. Emma was dismayed to see the boat's freshly washed paintwork blackened by the coal dust, which sifted even into the tightly closed cabin. But now there was no time to clean up.

"Emma Deane," Mrs. Minshull called, leaning over the side of the boat. She had something in her hand, which she passed to Emma. It was a bonnet of blue-sprigged cotton, like Mrs. Minshull's black one, with a stiff quilted brim and a crown of frills and a long lace-edged curtain in back to shield her neck from the sun.

Emma gazed at the bonnet in her hand, her mouth open. She had noticed Mrs. Minshull sewing something in the evenings by the lantern's light, but she had not dreamed it was for her.

"Put it on, lass. Put it on! Dinna stand there gawpin'. We mun get ahead!" cried Mrs. Minshull. She waved Emma forward with an impatient shake of her hand. Her face looked cross.

Emma raised the bonnet and set it on her head, the brim pushed forward over her eyes and the strings untied to dangle on her shoulders as Mrs. Minshull wore hers.

"Oh, Mrs. Minshull," she breathed.

"Aye, aye. Get along wi' ye!" said Mrs. Minshull.

Emma tugged on Rosie's harness.

"Go it, girl!" she cried, and the boat began slowly to move away from the coal yard dock, swimming low in the water, as the horse leaned into her collar.

Emma straightened her back and stepped out, one booted foot before the other. In the shade of the bonnet's brim, she could open her eyes wide against the sun's glare, and she looked along the towpath with a thrill of anticipation. She knew she looked like a real boatwoman now, clean right through to the skin, her hair neatly plaited beneath her jaunty bonnet, her feet sturdily shod.

What would she meet, she wondered, around the next bend of the cut?

# GETTIN' AHEAD

IN THE COMING DAYS, they took coal to the barges at Preston Banks and picked up lumber for the building of a new saltworks at Middlewich. They carried wheat to flour mills and sacks of flour from them—"Me father were a miller," said Mrs. Minshull. They hauled stones and bricks and sand. But sometimes, between loads, there was a day or two without work, and Emma noticed how Mrs. Minshull fretted and eked out their food until they were busy again.

The primroses under the hedges died away, and the wild hyacinths sprang up. Oxeye daisies and purple-and-white clover carpeted the meadows. Dog roses and honeysuckle festooned the hedges, and the bees reeled about them as though they were drunk.

If Emma thought of her old life as she perched on a balance beam waiting for a lock to empty or fill, she thought of it with dismay. It seemed to her she had dragged through those years half dead, with only the flick of the steward's cane to rouse her. If Nancy dinna need me . . . , she thought.

She could see that her thin white arms were filling out and growing brown. She could feel her legs grow stronger, her lungs expand to breathe the wholesome air.

Now she usually had plenty to eat. Yet instead of growing less hungry, it seemed to Emma that her appetite grew. She learned to eat the young green shoots from the hawthorn hedges along the towpath—"bread and cheese," Mrs. Minshull called them. She began to hunt for birds' eggs along the way and, once in a while, ducks' eggs in nests hidden in the grass of caved-in banks. Always there was soup or stew, simmered from vegetables Mrs. Minshull bought from canal-side cottages, and sometimes a rabbit or a moorhen, slain with the sling kept close at hand upon the cabin roof. When work was plentiful, there was fruit and meat pies, purchased also from cottages, and bread. There was ale, foamed into their bucket by innkeepers, and tea brewed by the cabin stove. Once there was even milk, nicked from a bawling cow at dusk. "We be doin' the poor creature a boon," said Mrs. Minshull. "The farmer should have milked her long sin'."

At night they moored near inns or farmhouses with stables to let. Once in a while, if the night was especially fine, Mrs. Minshull draped Rosie in her blanket, and they moored by a bridge in the fields.

But the weather was not always fine. Some days

dawned gray and wet. Emma tramped through drizzles and through downpours of rain, Mr. Minshull's old waterproof tenting her head. Once when it thundered, Mrs. Minshull sheltered the stern of the boat beneath a bridge and called Emma to join her on board. They sat cozily in the cabin, listening to the rain beat upon the top sheets, and drank hot tea while Mrs. Minshull crocheted. Mrs. Minshull often crocheted of an evening or as she steered on the long, straight stretches, the tiller under her arm.

She grew no more garrulous, but now, sometimes at the end of the day, she got out a deck of playing cards, limp with age and use, and taught Emma cribbage. Keeping score, Emma began to learn her numbers in a way she never had at Sunday school. The old woman also started showing Emma the intricate crochet stitches. She gave Emma a hook of her own. Once, her voice high and cracked, Mrs. Minshull sang the old song "Barbara Allen" and taught Emma the refrain.

They plied up and down the cut, back and forth to Manchester, over to Ellesmere Port, to Wigan and Chester and Barbridge. But they did not go to Macclesfield again.

Was it by design, Emma wondered. She had ceased long since asking the old woman how to get home, but she knew, uncomfortably, that she ought to go if the chance arose.

How did Nancy fare, without Emma's help and wages? Did she weep for her at night, when Ben had gone to the inn? Most like, by now, she thinks I be dead,

Emma thought, and the thought was almost a comfort. It came to her that perhaps it was as well.

"I heared ye've a load fer me," said Mrs. Minshull.

But the foreman of the saltworks wharf did not even turn to look at her as he said, "Aye, missus, so I did, but Josiah Tubbs were here afore ye, and it could na wait."

Emma watched Mrs. Minshull's face anxiously. It had been five days this time since they had a load, though Mrs. Minshull had inquired at every shipping office and wharf along the way, and twice, as now, they had gone a fool's errand, seeking cargoes that had been snatched from beneath their noses.

Are we na gettin' ahead fast enough, Emma longed to ask the old woman, but Mrs. Minshull did not speak to her of the business of the boat, and it was only by watching and listening that Emma learned as much as she knew.

Now she saw Mrs. Minshull's lips tighten and her eyes spark with annoyance.

"Get along, lass," she called to Emma, reaching over the side to flick their rope from the bollard. Emma tugged on Rosie's bridle.

"Ye might try the Lion Saltworks at Marston on Monday," tossed the foreman over his shoulder. "They've a tidy lot o' shippin' o' late. But th'owners be chapel folk. They'll na start a boat o' the Sabbath."

It was Saturday afternoon. Emma had noticed they needed a new towrope, for the old one had been spliced so many times it looked like a string of rags. But Mrs.

Minshull had made no move to replace it, so perhaps her purse was near empty. The next load's fees must be saved, come what may, Emma had learned, for the canal owners exacted a price from the boatmen for the use of the cut. Emma was beginning to realize the sacrifice Mrs. Minshull had made when she bought Emma's boots. She was not so rich as Emma had supposed, for the boat required a good bit of maintenance, and, of course, Rosie must be kept. Emma had started watching to make certain the old woman had eaten her fill before she asked for second helpings. She noticed that, clean as they were, Mrs. Minshull's clothes were patched and threadbare. Now that Emma wore one of her gowns, they had but one change between them, and Mrs. Minshull insisted they change their clothes every fortnight or so. They took turns wearing the clean gown and washed a dirty one whenever they had the chance.

The boat pulled away from the Middlewich wharf. Emma wondered if Marston was far away. Perhaps they might reach it before evening and take on a load before the pious owners of the Lion Saltworks closed their wharf. Emma liked carrying salt. It did not dirty the boat as coal did and could be stacked in the hold in its tidy white blocks without so much fear of shifting.

But they did not reach Marston that evening. They passed through the flat, factory-scarred landscape of Middlewich, with its mean rows of workers' cottages beside the cut, and through a series of three narrow locks and then a single big one and so into a wide, lock-free stretch of canal that wound for some distance along the side of a hill as it followed a peaceful river valley.

Emma thought about the country folk she saw working about the scattered farmsteads and hamlets along the way. She had a vague memory that her mother and father had come to Macclesfield from the country many years ago. That was why they liked to take the children walking in the countryside at infrequent holiday times. Emma thought her father had once had his loom in his country cottage in the days before the mills.

But the thought of her mother and father brought Nancy to mind, and Emma's thoughts veered away. She did not want to wonder whether the baby had died yet, whether Nancy had gone back to the mill, whether Ben was taking out on her his anger and despair.

They came to Northwich near dusk and found a moorage beside a bridge. While Mrs. Minshull went to inquire after loads, for Northwich too was a salt town, Emma stabled Rosie at the nearby inn. Then Emma went back to the boat and climbed aboard. She thought she would make their tea while she waited for Mrs. Minshull to return.

But she was surprised to find that the larder cupboard under the tiller was almost bare. There was only the end of a loaf of bread and a nubbin of cheese scarcely large enough for one. She had found no eggs that day, nor had Mrs. Minshull stoned a rabbit. In the tea caddy, there was but a few broken leaves and dust. They would have to wait to visit the shops when the old woman returned, Emma thought . . . if there was any money.

For a time, while the dusk deepened, Emma sat on the stern and waited for Mrs. Minshull. Beside the *Cygnet* was moored another boat and its butty, and she watched through the open cabin door as the ample boat-woman stirred something on the shelf of her bottle stove. She was talking to her children, who sat, Emma imagined, on the side bed. Emma could hear their voices, a sort of cozy sound, though she could not make out the words.

"What concerns them dinna concern ye," Mrs. Minshull would say if she caught Emma listening to or watching another boat family. For all their friendliness, the boat folk kept to themselves. It was as though each boat were surrounded by an invisible wall that they pretended shut out the world.

"Hi ho, Ma!" came a voice, and Emma saw a boy climb aboard the neighbor boat. He held up a string of shining fish in the light of their cabin lantern.

She heard the squeal of delighted children's voices and saw the woman take the fish from his hand.

"Now there be a lovely tea, George," the woman said. "I'll fry 'em up an' all."

Fish. That would make a tea for her and Mrs. Minshull too, Emma thought, and no money spent. She and Mrs. Minshull had sometimes fished in the canal while waiting for a load. But the boy's fish were larger and fatter than the fingerlings they had caught. If she could find Mrs. Minshull's fishing line and hooks, she'd ask the boy where he had caught them. She'd take the lantern. She'd heard that fish would come to a light at night.

By the time Emma had found the fishing gear, the smell of frying fish was coming across the water, so pungent it made Emma's mouth water. Deliberately, she looked through the invisible wall to where the boy sat on his cabin roof and held up her light so he could see her face in the now deep darkness.

"Where did ye cotch the fish?" she called. "I've a taste fer a mess meself."

The boy jerked his head in surprise. Emma knew he had not noticed her before.

"Eh?" he said, and then waved his arm vaguely in the direction of the town. "Oh, yon, in the river."

"Thank ye kindly," Emma said.

She could feel the boy's curious eyes upon her.

"'Tis late fer fishin'," he said.

"Aye."

Emma pulled the boat to the bank by tugging on the rope. Then she stepped ashore and set out in the direction the boy had indicated.

# A Light in the Dark

AT FIRST THE WAY TO THE RIVER WAS CLEAR—a long, narrow street that led away from the canal. The street was lined with shops, darkened now. Only an occasional lighted upper room cast a faint iridescence upon the puddled street below. Emma breathed through her mouth as she hurried along. How had she lived so long in a town and never noticed the stink?

But, abruptly, the street came to an end. Which way, Emma wondered. She wished there were someone to ask, but the street was empty. She chose the right-hand way, for she thought she glimpsed something that might be a bridge in the distance. The river, the boy had said.

It was not a bridge, but only the railing of a church-yard. Once again, Emma paused, undecided. Once again, she chose a turning.

A cat yowled, making Emma jump and drop her lantern. It snuffed out. When she straightened from picking it up, she saw ahead the glow of lighted windows and hurried toward it. She would ask the way, she thought, and have her lantern lit.

But the windows belonged to an inn—not a friendly canal-side inn such as she was accustomed to, with its door open wide to show the innkeeper, flushed and jolly behind his scrubbed bar, but a low, mean place, a place like the one Ben frequented. Emma could hear the roistering voices within, and they sounded harsh and threatening. Of a sudden, the door burst open, and three men reeled into the street, one of them retching. Emma flattened herself against a wall and watched, her heart in her throat, as the man vomited on the cobbles. The other men laughed and pulled him away down the street.

When they were gone, Emma wrenched herself from the wall and scrambled away in the opposite direction. She could hear the raucous shouting from the inn. Against her will, her legs began to churn faster and faster beneath her skirts. Her heart seemed suddenly to burst, and she broke into a run. Her head turned from side to side. She had forgotten it was the river she searched for. She wanted only the boat. But where was the canal? Down this dark way, or that? The clang of a church bell set her head spinning. A pack of dogs turned her from her path. She fled from them blindly, running.

She did not stop until her legs gave way. Gasping, she dropped down on the doorstep of a darkened building and painfully began to gather her thoughts. The moon was rising, and it shed its pale glow over the street, making still darker the shadows. It was a street of warehouses, Emma saw. They loomed over her, huge and silent. There was only one light, in a window high above. Emma lifted her head, wondering if she dared pound on that warehouse door to ask the way. She drew a deep breath . . . and smelled water, the cool, dank smell of water.

Emma pulled herself up and tottered in the direction of the smell, through a narrow alley between two warehouses. When she stepped out of the alley, she was on a stone wharf, flooded with moonlight. It was the canal!

A smile stretched her mouth, and her heart lifted. She realized that she still clutched Mrs. Minshull's lines and hooks, along with the dark lantern, and felt glad. She would look for the river again in the morning, she thought, and they would have fish for breakfast. Now she wanted only to find the *Cygnet* and Mrs. Minshull.

But which way did they lay?

To the left was a footbridge over the canal. Emma did not remember seeing a footbridge as they entered the town. But had she been paying mind? The bridge against which they had moored was a wide one, wide enough for wagons. They had passed warehouses much like these, Emma remembered. But were they the same warehouses, or only ones that looked the same?

Emma felt her lower lip tremble and caught it between her teeth. Think, she told herself. Think. But her mind would not move, except in circles.

She craned her head to the right. There was a light to the right, far down the cut. It seemed to be at a place where the canal opened into a boatyard, and Emma could see on the water several long shadows—narrowboats.

Not *Cygnet*, but they *were* narrowboats like her, with boatmen who, Emma thought, could be trusted to help. She began to walk swiftly toward the light.

The light was on a narrowboat drawn up upon a dry dock. Emma could see that the boat was new built. Everything about it was clean and unscathed—even the shining black hull.

A man knelt on the boat, a lantern beside him. He held a paintbrush in his hand and squinted at the half-painted surface. He seemed unaware of Emma, coming up behind him, as he leaned forward to paint a stroke. Then, of a sudden, he reared back.

"Och! Fool that I be!" he exclaimed, and reached for a rag to rub out what he had done.

"Beggin' yer pardon," Emma said.

The man whirled, startled, and his brush strewed drops of paint after it.

"Now see what ye've made me do!" he cried. "There's a proper muddle!"

"Oh, I do beg yer pardon, sir," Emma said. "I dinna mean to mither ye. I wanted only to ask me way."

The man's face softened.

"Och, nay, lass," he said. "'Tis na yer fault. I be fagged out, and the light is na good. I were makin' a fair muddle o't afore e'er ye spake." He sighed and rubbed at the paint splotches with his rag. "What be a little lass like yerself doin' out alone i' the night?"

"I were seekin' the river, only I lost me way, and now I dinna know where me boat lies," Emma said, coming up close to him and reaching to rub out a paint spot with her apron.

"Be ye off a narrowboat then?"

"Aye, the *Cygnet*. I be Mrs. Minshull's huffler."

"Oh, aye, I heard o' Bob Minshull's passin'. So Granny's taken on a girl to crew, has she?"

Emma nodded.

"We come from Middlewich and moored at a wagon bridge close by some warehouses," she said. "Only now I be so turned about, I dinna know whether it be this way or that."

The man gave a final rub with his cloth and straightened up. He groaned and put his hand to his back as he surveyed his work.

"That looks like Dick's hatband what went halfway 'round and tucked," he said, shaking his head. "I ne'er will be finished by Monday, though I canna do more tonight."

He cleaned his brush on the rag and began putting the lids on his paint pots.

"Rest awhile by," he said, "and I'll take ye to yer boat. I know the place. A little lass should na be wanderin' alone so late."

❖    ❖    ❖

His name was Isaac Morton, and he built narrow-boats with his old father, who was Isaac Morton also. This much Emma learned on the walk back to the *Cygnet*. Emma had to skip to keep up with his stride, but his gruff, warm voice pulled her along beside him in the glow of her lantern, which he had lit from his own and which he carried for her. The boat he was painting had been commissioned by a small boat company, he said. It was promised for the following Monday. "But me dad took sick, and I could na find help, so I'm sore behind-hand. 'Tis me dad does the fancy paintin'. I be all thumbs wi' such nigglin' work."

As they went, Isaac Morton pointed out to Emma the way to the river that she had missed. "Just along that street to its end, then turn left," he said.

In a few more steps, the *Cygnet* was in sight, moored with its neighbor beside the wagon bridge.

"Thought ye'd buggered off like that Tom," was all the old woman said when Isaac delivered Emma aboard, but Emma saw that she had been fretted.

She be glad to have me back, Emma thought. She be *glad*, and na only fer me help. It be fer meself. Emma did not know how she knew this, but she did. It be somethin' in her eye what tells me, Emma thought as she told of her search for the river, of getting lost, of finding Isaac Morton, who helped her at last.

"It were na mither," Isaac said, tipping his hat to Mrs. Minshull before he strode away.

It was the next morning, by full light, that Emma

found herself returning from the river along the way Isaac Morton had shown her, a string of fish in her hand. Her stomach felt flat and empty, yet she was strangely satisfied. Perhaps it was the prospect of a fish breakfast before her, or perhaps it was the memory of Mrs. Minshull's face last evening when Isaac brought her back.

She was in sight of the *Cygnet* when Emma thought to take a fish to Isaac Morton. To say thank ye, she thought, fer bringin' me home. She ran the last few steps to the boat and jumped aboard.

"Here be breakfast, missus," she cried, flinging down the fish upon the top of the larder cupboard. "I'll be back afore they be fried."

Mrs. Minshull poked her head out of the cabin.

"Good lass," she said, and Emma thought that perhaps she smiled.

Emma selected the largest, fattest fish.

"This be fer Mr. Morton," she told the old woman, and was off, running down the towpath before Mrs. Minshull could reply.

Emma found Isaac Morton where she had found him the night before, crouched on the new narrowboat, paintbrush in his hand. He was swearing.

"I canna fer the life o' me make these di'monds neat," he said, catching sight of Emma. "What I'll do fer the roses an' castles, I dinna know."

"I brought this fer ye," Emma said shyly, holding out the fish.

Isaac Morton wiped his brush and put it down. Then he took the fish, turning it this way and that in the sunlight.

"Now then," he said. "Ain't it a fine one!" He heaved a sigh. "Me wife'll cook it fer me tea," he said.

He unbent his long body and walked with the fish to the canal's edge. There he tied it to the dock with a piece of string to dangle in the water.

"It'll keep there," he said, "'til she brings me noonday meal."

Emma had trailed him to the canal. Now she trailed him back to the dry dock and watched as he took up his brush once again. Her own fish was frying back on the *Cygnet* this very moment, she thought. Still, she was loathe to leave the boatbuilder. She stood behind him and watched as he dipped his brush into the red paint. He was trying to paint a simple diamond shape, but Emma could see his brush wavered on what should have been the clean, sharp edge of it. What was the trouble, she wondered. In every other way, he seemed so sure and able. She could feel her own hands twitching at her sides.

I could do it, she thought, tracing the line of the diamond's edge in her mind. She remembered watching Mrs. Minshull repaint her cabin-door roses. She remembered designs and pictures she herself once sketched on her Sunday school slate. She remembered the flowers she had traced in the dust. Diamonds were easy, compared to flowers.

"I could do it," she heard her voice say softly, and she blushed.

"Eh?" said Isaac Morton.

*Cygnet* was not going to Marston today after all. Mrs. Minshull had been late last evening because she had been arranging a cargo to be picked up Monday morning right here in Northwich. "We'll have a bit o' holiday," she had said, "and do some fettlin' o' the cabin."

So now Emma took a deep breath and cleared her throat.

"Mayhappen I could help," she said, her voice growing stronger, "if Mrs. Minshull can spare me."

# BIRDIE

An hour later, her stomach full and her mouth still tasting of fried fish, Emma squatted where Isaac Morton had been earlier and dipped a brush into the pot of red paint. Carefully she wiped the brush free of excess paint against the pot's rim as she had seen Mrs. Minshull do. Then she drew the paint-filled bristles along the wavering edge of Isaac Morton's diamond in a sure, straight line. Behind her, Isaac and Mrs. Minshull let out their held breaths simultaneously.

"She do have a steady hand," said Isaac.

"Aye," said Mrs. Minshull. "That she do."

Emma thought she heard pride in the old woman's voice, but she was afraid to look around at her face. Gently she stroked on the shining red to fill the diamond.

"This'd be white, methinks," she ventured when she was finished, pointing with the brush handle to a half-diamond chalked above the red one. "And this and this, but I'll make these red and these blue, if it pleases ye."

"Aye, and aye again," exclaimed Isaac Morton. "Just what I had in me mind. Me old dad could na plan it better, and he be paintin' boats for nigh fifty year."

"Where did ye learn, lass?" said Mrs. Minshull. "I dinna know ye were handy."

Emma shrugged. She had never before that moment held a paintbrush in her hand, but she had gotten her fingers smacked with a ruler for drawing pictures on her Sunday school slate instead of copying her letters. And she remembered now her game with colored threads on the floor of the weaving loft. She used to make designs of them, and pictures, and patterns in pretty colors that Mother had admired. It was not painting, but it had made her feel then as she felt now—soothed and happy, the images forming and re-forming in her mind while her hands made them real.

"Mayhappen she'll be a pattern maker," her mother had said. It was something that Emma had forgotten— that long-ago ambition of her mother's. Silk pattern makers were elite among factory hands. They sat in the offices on the top floor, with braziers in winter to keep their fingers supple, and drew their lovely designs on paper.

Yet, thinking of it now, Emma shuddered. Even pattern makers must work in the mill. She would rather by far lead Rosie along the cut's towpath.

She looked up suddenly, her brush pausing in its

work as she twisted around to anxiously examine Mrs. Minshull's face.

"Be ye certain ye can spare me?" she asked.

"Aye, lass. We've more need of yer earnin's today than yer toil. 'Tis kind o' Mr. Morton to offer ye wages."

"Na such thing," said Isaac Morton. "The lass be the answer to me prayers."

Emma turned back to her painting. Mrs. Minshull still needed her, she assured herself.

Emma thought often of that day in the weeks that followed. As she led Rosie beside heavy-scented privet hedges abuzz with bees and past purple stands of foxglove and loosestrife and rosebay willow herb, she noted the graceful way the wildflowers nodded on their stems and regretted the stiffness of the flowers she had painted for Isaac Morton on the cabin panels of the new narrowboat. Passing lock cottage gardens, she studied the colors of roses and hollyhocks and sweet williams and the way the leaves of woodbine grew trained up against a wall. In her mind she traced the shapes of trees and bridges and buildings, memorizing them should she ever have a chance to paint a castle scene like those on the doors of some boats. Isaac Morton had said that her pictures were "lifelike," but Emma wished she had done better. When she had a moment, she practiced drawing with a stub of charcoal on shingles or flat rocks she found along the way and, later, on the blank backs of old toll tickets.

"Dost ye know how to write?" she once asked Mrs.

Minshull, thinking of the fancy lettering that Isaac had traced onto the panels of the boat cabin.

But the old woman had said, "Nay."

Mrs. Minshull did not comment on Emma's "scribblin's," as Emma thought of them, but it was she who gave Emma the bundle of used-up toll tickets from the ticket drawer and she who presented Emma with a stubby paintbrush and three half-gone pots of paint.

"No doubt ye'll find a use fer these," she had said briskly, turning away so Emma could not thank her. "But I'll na have ye slackin'. Ye'll do yer work first!"

"Oh, I will, Mrs. Minshull. I will!" Emma had assured her.

The weather that July was close and sultry, brilliant sun alternating with torrents of rain. Emma was often wet to the skin as she walked the towpath, and so was Rosie, her crocheted cap drooping into her eyes, almost as bothersome as the flies it was meant to deter.

It was on such a rainy afternoon that Emma's eye was caught by the fluttering of the ivy leaves that grew close beside the path at the foot of a tree.

"Gee up," she said to Rosie, and gently slapped the horse's flank. Then Emma stepped quietly over to the tree to see if she had chanced upon something good to eat for tea—an injured rabbit that needed putting out of its misery or a bird on a nest of eggs. She knelt and parted the ivy with her hands, but in the shadow of the tree, she could spy nothing against the brown earth. She started to rise, then heard a rustle and looked once again.

It was a bird, no larger than the palm of Emma's hand, that crouched, shivering, against the wet ivy leaves. Emma felt its sharp black eyes fixed on her. Its outsize beak yawned open and closed, but made no sound. For a moment only, Emma considered whether the bird was suitable for eating, but then something about its helpless shivering went to her heart.

"Poor little mite," she crooned, advancing her hands toward it. "Poor little birdie, be ye cold and wet? Why dinna ye fly into the tree to dry yerself under the leaves?"

The beady eyes stared at her, and the tiny bedraggled body trembled, but the bird did not fly. Instead, much to Emma's surprise, for it did not seem to be injured, it submitted to the closing of Emma's fingers around it and nestled into her hands when she lifted it to her face. For a moment she held it to her cheek, feeling the wild beating of its heart. Then, swiftly, she rose and tucked it into her apron pocket. The boat was passing, and Mrs. Minshull was shouting from the stern for her to go on.

"Ye'll dry soon enough in there, Birdie," Emma said, holding pocket and bird carefully away from the bumping of her legs as she ran to catch up to the horse.

For the rest of the afternoon, Emma was intensely aware of the tiny movements and soft sounds from the bottom of her deep apron pocket. She half expected the bird to emerge suddenly and take wing, once it was dry and warm, but instead, for a time, she thought that it had died, it lay so still. Peeking, she saw that its eyes were closed, but its little breast trembled with breath.

"Poor little Birdie," she found herself singing softly, as though in lullaby.

"See, Mrs. Minshull, what I found," she cried as she climbed into the cabin at teatime.

The little bird was cupped in her hands, held out to the old woman. Mrs. Minshull peered through the steam billowing from the teakettle.

"A wee fledglin'," she said. "Did it fall from its nest?"

Emma looked curiously at the bird.

"I reckon," she said. "I found him wet in th'ivy, and he dinna fly away."

Mrs. Minshull smiled.

"Nay, lass, it canna. It be too young. Were there na mother bird asquawkin' thereabouts?"

Emma shook her head.

"Then *ye* mun be its mother 'til it be old enough to fend fer itself."

"Me?" Emma looked into the old woman's face in wonder. "But I dinna know how to nurse a bird. What'll he like to eat? Where mun he sleep?"

But Mrs. Minshull had already opened the door in the rear of the cabin and was rummaging in the storage space in the hold.

"This'll do," she said, turning back with a wicker cage in her hand. "Once, Mister found a wee turtledove wi' a broken wing. He fashioned this fer it. Ye can put yer bird here and feed it on snails and berries. There be rucks o' them about this time o' year."

"Snails?" said Emma.

The old woman cackled at her tone.

"Aye, thrushes eat snails, I'll be bound, and worms. The dove was less mither—it liked Rosie's grain well enough."

"He be a thrush then?"

"Aye, it do look a song thrush to me."

Emma stroked the baby bird with one finger as she put it through the little door of the cage. It settled on the floor, stretching out its wings and craning its head. Its wide-open mouth cried aloud.

"It be beggin' right now fer a great fat snail or two, I'll be bound," said Mrs. Minshull, turning to the stove.

From that day, Emma was even busier. Besides her duties to Mrs. Minshull and Rosie, and her "scribblin's," she must keep a sharp eye out for snails, clinging to the grass stems at the water's edge, or for worms wiggling up through the mud on wet mornings, or for the occasional red rowanberry or ripe bilberry or, rarely, a last wild strawberry other birds had missed.

Birdie was always hungry, opening his beak with plaintive, insistent cries whenever he caught sight of her. He grew bigger every day, she thought, noting the way his wings were feathering and the fluff atop his head was smoothing into a sleek olive-brown cap. Soon he could crush his snails for himself against the cage floor, and one evening Emma saw him catch a moth, attracted by the lantern. He began to sing when, on sunny days, his cage was set atop the cabin roof.

By then, blackberries were plentiful, hanging heavy and sweet on the path-side brambles. Emma gathered them in a basket as she walked, not just for Birdie's dinner, but for Mrs. Minshull's and her own. Goldenrod and red poppies and harebells waved in the meadows, and Emma saw farmers haying in the fields.

Evenings there was a chill in the air that made Emma look forward to snuggling on her side bed, warm beside the stove. Birdie would chuckle quietly in his cage, and Mrs. Minshull would show her a new crochet stitch. Emma was learning them quickly.

"Ye've clever fingers," said Mrs. Minshull, and Emma's cheeks warmed to the praise.

It was only those rare nights when Emma did not fall instantly asleep that she found herself thinking of Nancy. I should have left th'old woman long sin', she fretted. But she needs me, Emma told herself, to get the boat ahead. Besides, they had not yet come to Macclesfield. How could I find me way, she thought, pulling the clean blanket up under her chin and trying to shut away the memory of the dirty rags Nancy slept in beside the cottage hearth.

So, it was a shock, one day in early September when they had loaded coal at a place called Kidsgrove, for Emma to hear a boatman tell Mrs. Minshull, "I've a load fer Macclesfield."

Mrs. Minshull did not look at Emma as she replied, "We be fer Burton-on-Trent."

"Mayhappen ye'll pick up a cargo o' ale there," the man said encouragingly, but Mrs. Minshull had turned hurriedly away and was busy with some rope work.

"Mayhappen," she said.

# THE WALL

THE BOAT WITH A LOAD FOR MACCLESFIELD had gone ahead of them through the last lock at Kidsgrove. As Emma waited for the lock to refill, she watched the boat turn sharply to the right off the main canal. It disappeared under a bridge.

If I followed that boat, I should soon be home, Emma thought.

Home. The word did not seem fitting.

But it *were* home fer all o' me life, Emma thought. And Nancy were good to me always. Ben . . .

Ben had tried to do his best by her, Emma admitted to herself. Until he was laid off and had taken to the drink, he had been kind to her in his way.

He meant fer me to go to the Chapel school, Emma remembered. He dinna aim fer me to work so long in the mill.

The lock was full, and Emma leaned hard against the

balance beam, walking backwards as the gate swung open to admit the *Cygnet*, with Mrs. Minshull standing in the stern, avoiding Emma's eye. Birdie was trilling sweetly from the cabin roof. Rosie leaned into her collar, knowing without being told that it was time to pull.

Home. It was the boat that now felt like home to Emma—the gaily painted *Cygnet* and Mrs. Minshull and Rosie and Birdie. It was they who needed her.

Only . . . she did not know whether Nancy and the baby also still needed her.

Lacking me wages, they may be clemmed to death by now, Emma thought. Surely the baby had died. And it were me fault, Emma thought, hanging her head.

"Wind down! Wind down!" Mrs. Minshull was shouting, and Emma jumped, startled from her thoughts. "Look sharp, me lass, or ye'll feel the weight o' me stick!" the old woman yelled. She was shaking her fist.

Emma ran to wind down the rear paddles while the boat settled forward in the lock.

What stick, she wondered. Mrs. Minshull had never struck her, with stick or fist or boot. But Ben had struck her many a time and kicked her too. Not Nancy, of course. Nancy had never hit her.

'Tis Nancy what be me sister, Emma thought as she trotted forward to let the water out of the lock. 'Tis Nancy what cared fer me when Mother and Father died and vowed she'd ne'er leave me. Nor did she. 'Twas me left her, Emma thought.

While her hands worked and the boat sank in the emptying lock, Emma's mind was racing. The other boat would soon be far ahead. Still, the canal arm down which it had gone must lead to Macclesfield. If she went straight on with the *Cygnet*, she would be going the wrong direction. Yet . . . how could Mrs. Minshull get ahead without her? This load of coal was expected in Burton-on-Trent in two days' time, and it would be a near thing as it was. Emma knew they had been late too often.

As Emma led Rosie down the sloping track to the lower level of the canal, the horse stretched her neck to nuzzle her. Emma could not help but smile, even in her distraction.

"Leave off, ye ol' silly," she said, patting the horse's nose before she left her to open the bottom gates.

How could I e'er have been feared o' her, Emma wondered, her eyes resting fondly on the great dappled horse. Rosie was watching Emma too. She nickered softly, her pink lips pulling back from her long yellow teeth.

The old woman could find another huffler, Emma told herself. Though Rosie might miss her, Mrs. Minshull wouldn't. She be too contrary, Emma thought.

"Gee up," she said to Rosie, giving her flank a slap that raised the dust from her hide. Rosie strained forward to start the boat swimming from the lock, and Emma stepped out behind her.

Ahead was the canal arm and the bridge over it. Emma saw that she must take Rosie over that bridge and back down the towpath on the other side of the main channel. But if she did not go over the bridge with Rosie, but instead turned right and doubled back, she would be following the canal arm to Macclesfield. She could feel Mrs. Minshull's eyes sharp upon her and, of a sudden, at the foot of the bridge, she made a sign that she needed to go into the bushes. She saw Mrs. Minshull hesitate, then nod, and Emma ducked behind a hedge. She parted its branches to watch the boat glide past.

Mrs. Minshull, tiny, erect, her eyes fixed on the water ahead, stood in the stern, her brown gnarled hand on the tiller. She looked very small to Emma.

Wee and nesh, Emma thought, wanting to start from her cover and run forward to Rosie's flank. But she could hear Birdie's song from the cabin roof—it seemed to Emma to be sung to the rhythm of Rosie's hooves—and she thought of Nancy singing to her babies, a soft mournful song so full of love and pain that Emma's heart used to ache to hear it. So Emma stayed where she was, her breath stopped in her mouth, until the boat was past.

Then, swiftly, she ran back along the way the Macclesfield boat had turned.

At first, Emma half hoped to hear Mrs. Minshull coming after her. As she ran, her ears strained for the sound of Rosie's hoofbeats behind her, for once or twice the old woman had climbed onto the horse's broad back to ride when she had a speedy errand. But there was no sound except the rap of a hammer from a nearby boat works.

When a pain began to catch at Emma's side, she slowed to a walk.

The canal arm led back parallel to the main channel, then crossed it on an aqueduct. From its height, Emma searched the cut below for the *Cygnet*, but the boat was already out of sight.

Emma moved on. In the distance behind some deserted buildings at the water's edge, she could see pottery works. Several times, she saw workmen carrying stacks of pots or great baskets filled with she knew not what. A boy ran past, his dirty bare feet thudding on the path.

Emma thought then of her boots and her gown and the bonnet that shaded her eyes. I should have left 'em wi' th'old woman, she thought. By rights they be hers, not mine. But it was too late. Now she'll know me a thief fer certain, Emma thought.

She trudged on, the water's quiet murmur in her ears, missing Birdie's trill, missing Rosie's whuffling breath, missing even the cursing of the old woman. When the path led through a cutting at the next lock, it seemed strange to Emma to pass without stopping to work the boat through.

With each step away from the *Cygnet*, Emma's heart grew heavier.

Be I dateless, she scolded herself. I ne'er had such grub, nor fine togs, nor soft bed. I ne'er had such pleasant work as here on the cut, nor such an easy master. What were I thinkin' of?

It was Nancy and the doubtless dead baby she had been thinking of. Will I go back to the mill then, Emma asked herself, recoiling from the thought.

And if they were all dead, what then? Mrs. Minshull would no longer want her, now she had proven herself the thief the old woman had always suspected. It be *me*'s buggered off now, Emma thought, remembering Mrs. Minshull's poor opinion of the fickle Tom. I've done fer meself now, Emma thought.

The sky was ruddy with the setting sun when Emma came in sight of a large town. Her belly pinched with hunger. Wearily she put one foot before the other. In all the long day's walk, she had known naught else to do. For she knew now that she had made a terrible mistake in leaving Mrs. Minshull. Yet something still drew her inevitably forward, out of the clean country air and into the smelly streets of the town. Away from the free gypsy life of the cut and toward the slavery of the mill. Away from Mrs. Minshull and Rosie and Birdie and toward Nancy and her baby . . . and Ben.

Emma passed a coal yard where several narrowboats were moored, ready for the next day's unloading. She thought she recognized the boat she had been following, but she could not be sure. Nothing else looked familiar.

"Missus," she ventured to a stout woman kneeling beside the canal, rinsing a horse's nose tin, "is't Macclesfield ahead?"

"Aye," said the woman in a civil tone, but she did not offer further information nor ask Emma whence she journeyed. Boat folk did not inquire into one another's business, Emma remembered.

As the houses pressed closer to the canal's edge and factories and warehouses began to loom above her, Emma's heart grew so heavy that she could scarce drag on. Her step faltered. She stopped to rest on the wall of a bridge and idly watched a boat go by in the dusk, longing as she had never longed before to catch up its horse's bridle and go with it. But the boy driving the horse was whistling as he walked and did not give Emma a glance. In a few moments, he was far down the path, his boat floating away as though in a dream.

Sighing, Emma heaved herself to her feet and stumbled on. Still nothing looked familiar, and then she remembered she was coming into Macclesfield from a different direction than the one she had taken when she left. She began to look for the door in the wall.

Even so, she almost went past it, so closely covered was it by the thicket that grew between it and the cut. The grass at the path's verge, which in spring had been sparse and pale, grew luxuriantly now. The bushes were deep green, almost black in the growing dark. She thought she must have missed the path to the gate when suddenly there it was—a narrow dusty track in the tall grass leading away from the cut.

Emma set her foot upon it and paused. She turned her head to look back at the water, silent and black now. Then she followed the track the few steps through the grass and into the thicket.

The wall cast a deep shadow, and Emma staggered a little, fending off branches with one hand and stooping to grope with the other. Her fingers met brick, and she stopped. She felt for the wood of the gate and found it, found the bolt and shot it. Then she pushed hard and heard the hinges grind and saw before her a faint light as the gate shuddered open.

# NANCY

THE NARROW WEAVER'S COTTAGE looked exactly as Emma had left it all those weeks ago.

Weeks? Emma thought, her hand upon the door latch. It had been months since she left by this same door to hurry to the mill. Spring it were then, she thought, and now it be almost autumn.

She could not bring herself to lift the latch. Instead, she stood in the shadow of the doorway and leaned her head against the door.

A candle flickered dimly through the dirty windowpane. It had been Nancy's custom to put a light in the window at night to guide Emma home from the mill, Ben from the public house. But from inside the cottage, no voice met Emma's ear, no clank of pots or scrape of chair . . . or cry of baby. Emma's stomach clenched.

Mayhap I should knock, she thought. But it seemed

strange to knock on a door she had entered time and again simply by lifting the latch.

From above her came a thumping and the screech of a curse. Emma turned and fled the doorstep, startled. After a few running steps, she halted, trembling, and looked back.

The sound had come from the loft. Emma could see shadows moving across the tall loft windows. An arm was upraised. Someone sobbed. It was all, all as it had been, Emma thought. Nothing had changed. The man upstairs still beat his wife. Doubtless Ben still beat Nancy.

Emma heard laughter from the cottage next door. Somewhere down the row, a door opened and closed, and someone hurried away, the sound of bare feet whispering on the brick-hard dirt of the street.

Doubtless old Maeve, the washerwoman, still swilled her gin. Doubtless Mrs. Mullins still dosed the neighbors' babes. Doubtless women and children still slaved in the mills. Doubtless men cursed and fought and drank.

Nothing, nothing had changed.

Saving me, thought Emma. I be changed from the worthless, hapless creature I were. I know a better life.

Emma hung her head. She felt a tear escape her eye and imagined it splashed on the dusty toe of her boot.

*Ye ne'er did flinch afore, lass!*

The voice in her mind was so real that for a moment Emma thought Mrs. Minshull had followed her after all. But a swift uplifting of her head and a scan of the empty street made her realize that she was only remembering the old woman's voice. As her pounding heart began to slow, she scrubbed at her eyes with her fist and drew a shuddering breath.

I dinna flinch at drivin' Rosie, she thought. I dinna flinch at the Marple locks. I dinna flinch at unloadin' coal, nor a long day's walk, nor at paintin' Mr. Morton's boat. I were a help to him and to Mrs. Minshull. I were even a help to Birdie. I reckon I can be a help to my own born sister.

Emma stepped quickly to the door again and put out a trembling hand. She lifted the latch.

A woman knelt by the hearth, her back to the opening door.

"Ben," she said. "Ye be right earl . . ."

As the woman swung around, her face smiling welcome, Emma saw her color drain away, her blue eyes widen. Nancy put out her hand, groping as though suddenly blinded by the vision of Emma standing in the doorway.

"'Tis but me, Nan," Emma said. "Be not afeared. 'Tis but me."

"Emma?" Nancy's voice sounded strange, as though she could not catch her breath. "Emma, be it truly thee?"

Then, of a sudden, a baby wailed.

Emma whirled toward the corner from whence the noise came.

"Be it alive then?" she said. "Oh, Nancy, has yer baby lived after all?"

"O' course he lives!" snapped Nancy, rising swiftly and

crossing the room to lift the baby from its pallet. "He be a big, strong mannikin, he be. His mammy's big, strong boy!"

Emma looked in wonder at her sister. Nancy's dress was as draggled and dirty as ever it had been. Her hair strayed from its knot, and there was a smudge of soot on her sunken cheek and a bruise on her chin. Her face was as thin, her bones as sharp as Emma remembered, but her eyes were blazing with life. She held out her skinny baby proudly.

"See how he thrives!" she cried. "He's got five teeth now and can gnaw a crust wi' the best. Friday last he took a step. No doubt he'll soon be walkin'. What did ye think, that he could na flourish wi'out his aunt Em?" And then Nancy's voice faltered. "Where ha' ye been, Emmy? I've looked and looked fer ye. I thought it was ye what was dead!"

"Oh," said Emma. "Aye . . ." She did not know what to say. "I be sorry if I've mithered ye, Nancy. I dinna mean to be away so long!"

"Emmy, Em!" Nancy cried, and in a moment Emma was fast held in her arms, along with the drooling baby, who looked into her face with round blue eyes and slobbered on her dress.

Nancy was crying now, Emma saw.

"Ach, the taters be burnin'," she cried suddenly, thrusting the baby into Emma's arms and whirling to the fire.

"Come to the hearth, sister dear," she said as she snatched up an iron spoon. "Pull up the cricket and sit ye down. I dinna mean to rail at ye. Only ye gave me a turn, walkin' in like that, and me givin' ye up months agone."

Ben did not, after all, come home early that night. Emma sat on the three-legged stool, and Nancy drew up the one rickety chair to the small, low flame and nursed her baby while Emma recounted her adventures. From time to time, Nancy reached out to touch Emma's hand or cheek, as though to reassure herself that Emma was truly there.

"Ye do look different, sister," she murmured. "Ye be so brown and stout, I scarce do know ye."

"I meant to come home that first eve," Emma kept saying. "I ne'er meant to be gone so long."

"Aye, aye," Nancy said, nodding as though she saw it all. She fingered the stuff of Emma's dress and examined Emma's bonnet, making soft sounds of wonder. The baby fell asleep on her lap.

When the potatoes were dry and falling to pieces, and still no sign of Ben, Nancy dished up portions for Emma and herself and poured them mugs of hot water.

"We'd as well sup," she sighed. "He must have stopped off wi' his chums."

"Has he got work?" Emma said. "How d'ye manage?" She meant, how do you manage without me?

"Oh, well enough. Well enough. He be workin' from time to time at Johnson's near Congleton. It be a fair walk, but they do say they'll be takin' on men full shifts, p'raps in a fortnight. I've gone back to the King Street Mill. D'ye mind Mag Jackson? She sees to our Benny while I be at work. A kindly soul she be."

Emma nodded slowly.

"Wi' me wages then," she said, "mayhappen we might prosper. D'ye think they'll take me back?"

"So ye've come home fer good?" Nancy said. She looked hard at Emma.

"Aye," Emma said, gazing at the filthy floor. Her head was aching. Perhaps it was the close, smoky air of the cottage or the smells of dirt and damp and unwashed bodies. Already her ankles were itching with flea bites and her scalp crawled. She longed for a good wash in Mrs. Minshull's basin.

"Th'old woman were cruel to ye?" Nancy said.

"Ach, nay," said Emma, smiling a little in spite of herself. "Her bark were worse than her bite."

"But the work be hard?"

"Na so very hard," said Emma.

"Ye dinna like the country then?"

Emma's voice sank lower. "I liked it right well," she said.

"Our people were country folk," said Nancy. "I mind Mother tellin' o' th'old village and the cottage where they bided when first they were wed."

Emma nodded. She did not remember, but Nancy was older and had known Mother better.

Nancy leaned forward and put a hand on Emma's knee.

"Emmy," she said. "Emmy, oh, Em . . . Ye had a chance! Why did ye come back?"

Emma's throat closed with the pain of the answer.

"I could na desert ye, Nancy," she whispered. "Ye'd ne'er have deserted me."

There were tears in Nancy's eyes as she cupped Emma's chin in her hand, but her voice was harsh.

"Ye canna do aught fer us, sister. Ye're but another mouth fer us to feed. On the morrow, go back to that old woman and beg her pardon. Ye take me blessin' wi' ye."

# FLINCHIN'

ONCE AGAIN, EMMA WAS WAKING to the baby's crying
and Nancy's voice trying to soothe it and Ben's cursing
as he staggered from his pallet, his head in his hands.
The scene was so familiar that, for a moment, Emma
thought Mrs. Minshull and the *Cygnet* but a lovely
dream.

So Ben did come home then, Emma thought. In her
exhaustion and despair the night before, she had slept so
deeply, despite the fleas in her blanket, that she had not
heard him. It mun have been late, she thought, for she
and Nancy had talked a long time. Nancy would not be
convinced, for all Emma repeated over and over the
impossibility of returning to Mrs. Minshull. "She'll
ne'er take me back," she had said. "Ye dinna know her."
Still, when Emma sank into sleep at last, it had been
beneath the weight of knowing that the gate to the
*Cygnet* was barred to her once and for all. There be

nothin' fer it but the mill, she had told herself. I shall be a help to Nancy whate'er she may say.

Now she sat up, pulling her shift straight, and clutched her blanket about her shoulders.

"Canna ye muzzle the brat?" Ben was crying.

"Muzzle yerself!" Emma was astonished to hear Nancy flash back. "He's as much right to make a wee noise as ye."

Nancy was bent over the hearth, blowing on the coals, her back to her husband, and Emma expected to see Ben rush at her, his thick hands flailing. But he only sank onto the chair with a groan.

Somewhat's awry here, Emma thought. Nancy ne'er used to speak so before, and if she had, she'd have paid fer it dearly.

Keeping Ben in view, Emma pulled on her gown and got to her feet. She began to edge toward the hearth to see what she could do to help. Nancy was rocking her baby in her arms and crooning to it while she waited for the water to boil.

Emma thought she was moving cautiously, but she must have caught Ben's eye, for suddenly his head reared back and he fixed his bleary gaze on her.

"So . . . ye've come back, ha' ye?" he croaked. "Did yer sluttin' ne'er put enough bread in yer belly that ye mun come crawlin' home again?"

"And where else would she come if she has a mind to? 'Twas *her* home long afore it were yourn!" snapped Nancy.

"Aye, an' who's paid the hire of it these last months?" shouted Ben, lurching to his feet. "I told ye she'd be back."

He staggered toward Emma, who cringed against the wall, and, before she could fend him off, he had given her the back of his hand.

Through a buzz of pain, Emma heard the sound Nancy made as she put the child behind her and scrambled to her feet.

"Leave off!" Nancy shouted. "Ye shall na strike her! Leave off, Ben. I be tellin' ye, leave off!"

Emma blinked back the stinging tears that had risen to her eyes. Her mouth throbbed, and she tasted the warm salt of her blood. She steeled herself for a second blow, but it did not come.

Ben had turned away from her, his shaggy head swinging like the head of a dancing bear Emma had seen once at the fair. He blundered toward Nancy, growling, then dropped to his knees, as though felled by an ax, and began to heave.

Emma watched in horror as the vile-smelling vomit spattered on the floor and steamed in the cool morning air.

"Be ye much hurted, Emmy?" Nancy was saying. She put her arm around Emma's shoulders. The baby was shrieking now.

Emma felt her teeth and wounded lips with her tongue. The teeth were still firm in her gums, the lips not badly torn.

"Nay," she said. "See to the baby. I be na hurt."

But Nancy snatched up Emma's boots and bonnet and shawl.

"Don these, and quickly," she said. "I canna keep him from ye fer long."

"But . . ."

Nancy was shoving her toward the cottage door.

"Go afore he comes to himself," she was saying. "Go back to yer mistress and yer boatin' life."

"But what about ye, Nan? What about the babe?" Emma cried.

Nancy stopped, for a moment, in her rush toward the door. The eyes she turned on Emma were bleak.

"We'll get by, Em. We'll get by. There be naught ye can do fer us. I do na take a thrashin' wi'out protest these days, and many's the time he be too drunk fer much harm. We need him, Benny and me, and I reckon he needs us. But you . . . you have a chance! I'll have comfort in the thinkin' o' ye on yer narrowboat."

Emma gaped at Nancy. She could hear Ben behind her, gasping.

"I could do worse, Emmy," Nancy was saying. "He be an honest man, and well meanin' fer all he canna stay away from the drink. Go, me dear, go!"

Then Emma was standing in the dawn-gray street, Nancy's kiss on her cheek, and Nancy was shutting the cottage door between them.

From inside, Emma could hear the screams of the baby. She heard Nancy calling to it.

"There now, Benny, hush ye. 'Tis only yer old da's makin' a fool o' himself. Hush, hush, hush."

Emma turned blindly from the door. She sank to the doorstep and began to lace her boots. Then she huddled there, in her shawl, her back to the firmly closed door behind which Nancy's life was going on—Wi'out me, Emma thought.

But she dinna understand, Emma thought. She may na need me, but neither do Mrs. Minshull.

The knowing rose in her throat as though to choke her, and she felt the tears rise too.

Home was not home after all. Her feelings had been right. Home was the boat, though she had not seen it.

And now I've deserted there too, Emma thought. Mrs. Minshull will have nabbed a new huffler by now. She'd have na need o' me e'en though she forgave me. Rosie'll forget me, and Birdie too.

The tears splashed on the bosom of her gown, making blacker spots on the rusty black. Emma did not bother to wipe them away. Her head sank to her knees in misery, and she gave herself over to crying.

Then, in the midst of her sorrow, a thought came that lifted her head and made her stare through her tears down the empty, squalid street.

I be flinchin', she thought. Whate'er would Mrs. Minshull say?

She'd say, *Pick yerself up, lass, and go on.* That's what she'd say.

But I dinna know where to go! Emma thought.

*Then ye be ne'er the lass I took ye fer.*

It was as though Mrs. Minshull were truly speaking to her. Emma stumbled to her feet and, with an effort, straightened her shoulders as befitted a boatwoman.

She set off for the canal.

She had had no breakfast, and tea last evening had been only those cooked-dry potatoes and a cup of hot water, but Emma was not thinking of food as she trotted through the dirty streets toward the wall and its gate. She was thinking of the canals, sketching their courses in her head, saying over to herself the names of the towns they had passed through, trying to remember their junctions and the locations of the shipping offices and the wharves where cargo might be loaded.

*Who do I know what might find me a boat to crew,* Emma asked herself. *Who would speak fer me?*

Isaac Morton. Though she had not seen him since she helped him to paint the new boat, he would remember what a good worker she was, how steady and ready in a pinch. But Emma could not sort in her mind the route to Mr. Morton's boatyard.

*It be at Northwich,* Emma remembered. *Northwich be after Middlewich. But where had they been before Middlewich? Where were they heading after?*

Emma wracked her brain. The route would not come clear. *Where was Northwich from Macclesfield? On what canal? How far?*

She unbarred the gate in the wall, almost without realizing what she was doing. She closed it after her and pushed through the brushy thicket. She was hurrying, and her breath came fast and her thoughts urgently. She was hurrying, hurrying . . . and then she was there, standing on the bank of the cut, where first she had seen the *Cygnet*.

The cut. Beside its shallow, slowly creeping water, Emma stopped, took a deep breath, and knew where to go.

Jock Nevins at the Marple locks. He was but a day's walk away. Jock Nevins would help her.

# JOCK NEVINS

It was midafternoon when Emma spied ahead of her the white balance beams of the top lock at Marple.

At last, she breathed to herself, as she forced one foot ahead of the other. Her knees trembled, and her heart hammered hard in her chest.

Had I but a sup o' food, I'd ne'er feel so weak, she told herself. But a bellyful of food would not still her terror. It had been a whole summer since that first encounter with the locks. Emma thought that Mrs. Minshull must have been purposely avoiding the Marples, lest Emma come too near Macclesfield, for they had never gone through them again. What if Jock Nevins were not there? What if there were a new lock keeper, someone who did not know her? Worse, what if Jock did not remember the girl he had taught about locks?

A boat was working through the first lock as Emma

came up to it. A surly-looking boatman and his dirty lad rushed from gate to gate, twirling the gears. Their butty waited its turn just below.

Company hirelin', Emma thought with disdain. She could not bring herself to ask such folk about Jock Nevins, though he was nowhere in sight. She descended the stone steps, wishing she had a stick to lean on, but she dared not venture from the path to seek one.

Below the third lock, she saw a figure on the path ahead. It was a man. That she could tell by the fork of his striding legs. But he seemed only a shadow, a moving slice of darkness that grew steadily near.

I shall ask that man, Emma resolved. She was having trouble lifting her feet, and the throb of her swollen face made it hard for her to think. Her head whirled, she stumbled, then found herself on her hands and knees, looking at the dirt of the path. She heaved herself to her feet and staggered forward a step or two, putting out a hand to steady herself. The man was quite close now, but still she could not make out his face.

"Mister?" Emma tried to say and heard a strange croaking sound. "Mister . . ."

She was squinting against the sunlight. Her bonnet had fallen back, and she could not seem to lift her hand to right it. The man's figure wavered. Emma's head spun. . . .

Then she was lying on the ground, supported by a strong arm beneath her shoulders, and a remembered voice was speaking to her from very far away.

"Missy . . . missy, can ye hear me? Missy?"

Emma opened her eyes.

Jock Nevins's face hung over her, his blue eyes creased with worry.

"Missy, can ye hear me?"

"Aye." This time Emma knew she had spoken, though her voice sounded faint and trembling.

"Be ye sick, missy?"

"Nay, only clemmed," Emma managed to say, and then all was dark again.

She woke to warm liquid in her mouth. She was swallowing, choking a little, and it tasted of tea, laced, as Ben's tea was often laced, with brandy.

"Can ye get down a crust o' bread, do ye think?" a woman's voice was saying.

Emma opened her eyes and saw the woman's face hovering above her. She did not know her but somehow knew instantly that the woman could be trusted. It was something in her dark eyes.

Emma struggled to lift her head. She was propped against pillows on a cot in a small, neat room, sunlit by an open doorway and a tiny curtained window. The woman sat beside her, a bowl and a spoon in her hands. Hurriedly, she put them down and leaned forward to help Emma sit up, plumping the pillows behind her.

"Be ye feelin' better then?" the woman said, and a deeper voice behind her cried, "Och, missy, an' it be a fright ye've given us!"

The man stepped forward.

"Jock Nevins!" Emma cried.

"So ye remember me?" he said, his brown face crinkling in a grin.

"I were lookin' fer ye," Emma said. "I . . ."

"Is't th'old woman? Do she be in trouble?"

Emma shook her head.

"I dinna know," she said. "I be na wi' th'old woman now. I . . . I left her yester morn."

"Left her?" said Jock Nevins.

Emma nodded, looking down at her hands, which were twisting in her apron. She could not meet his eyes.

"'Tis me what be in trouble," she said, almost whispering. "I need a place . . . on a boat. I know a good deal 'bout boats now, and as ye mind, I learn fast. Methought ye might know a boat what needs a huffler. . . ." Her voice trailed away. She could feel Jock Nevins's searching eyes on her bruised and swollen face.

"I ne'er would have thought she'd hit a wee lass," he said. "I knew she were rough-spoken, but I thought her heart were good."

"Oh, but it is!" cried Emma. "'Twas na Mrs. Minshull lammed me, but another . . . after . . . after I left her . . ."

She was looking at him eagerly now, anxious that he should not think ill of Mrs. Minshull, but her shame stopped her voice. She had not thought how she would explain her desertion of the old woman.

"Mayhappen ye'd best have a tell," Jock Nevins said, but the woman interrupted him.

"Mayhappen the child should sup," she said. "Time enough after fer tellin'."

It had all been told. Emma sat on the balance beam of the lock before Jock Nevins's cottage, her stomach full, but an empty feeling in her heart.

On the doorstep of the cottage sat Mrs. Nevins, for that was who the dark-eyed woman was. Her hands were busy with a bit of mending, and a baby, tied by a rope to the leg of her chair, crawled near her feet among the hare-bells and heartsease that grew by the walk. The golden sun slanted low, casting a honeyed light on the baby's halo of hair and on the water in the lock. Emma stared into the water and idly swung her leg.

"Dinna fear, missy," Mrs. Nevins was saying. "Jock'll think o' somewhat. Ye do leave it to Jock to find a way fer ye." She leaned down to take something from the baby's slobbery mouth. "Nay, Sissy, we dinna eat bugs."

"It were daft o' me to leave her," said Emma sadly. She sighed. "We were gettin' along, Mrs. Minshull and me. Rosie took to me, and I had a wee birdie in a cage and me own place on the side bed and . . ."

"Ye were mithered fer yer sister," said Mrs. Nevins in her comfortable voice. "Ye owed a duty to blood kin that ye could na deny. Did ye ne'er tell Mrs. Minshull 'bout Nancy? Did ye ne'er say what was in yer heart?"

Emma kicked her leg and hung her head.

"Nay," she said. "She were na one fer talkin', Mrs. Minshull."

"Aye, but na good comes from hidin' yer heart,

missy. I canna but think she would have been glad to know ye dinna *want* to leave her. She might have helped ye to get home fer a wee visit, had she but known."

Emma watched a cloud of gnats spin in a ray of sunlight. She nodded her head slowly, remembering that Mrs. Minshull *had* helped her when she knew what was wanting. She had given her boots and bonnet, paints and ticket backs to paint on and time too, when she was able.

"Mayhappen," Emma said. She could hear the hopelessness of the word. "It be too late now," she said.

"Leave it to Jock," said Mrs. Nevins. "Sissy, I told ye, na bugs in yer mouth. . . . Leave it to Jock, and dinna frab yerself."

"I canna go on eatin' yer grub, Mr. Nevins," Emma said. She and Jock were ambling along the towpath above the Marple locks, he with a scythe in his hand, she carrying on her shoulder his hooked bill on its long staff. They were trimming the hedges and the long grass to keep the path clear for traffic.

It had been a fortnight, and still Emma lingered at the lock cottage, pressed to stay by the kindly keeper and his wife. But the evenings were chilly now. The trees had turned, and leaves scudded before the wind and swirled in the weirs.

"There be Mr. Morton o' Northwich might know a place fer me," Emma said. "If ye mapped me the way, I know I could find him. I did a job o' work fer him once, and he seemed fair pleased. Then, at least I'd be earnin' me bread."

Jock Nevins shook his head.

"I was hopin' we'd hear somewhat from Mrs. Minshull," he said. "I've sent word to her by ev'ry boat agoin' Burton way."

His words struck Emma's heart like a blow. She had not realized that she had been hoping too, until he said it.

"She dinna want me back," she said, her voice low. "I did tell ye. Be there na other boat I could serve?"

"I have na heared tell o' one, missy," said Jock Nevins. "But dinna frab yerself. Ye be na trouble to us."

Emma knew that she *was* trouble. There was little enough to be stretched to feed Jock Nevins's growing family, without her. The two toddling babes had been turned from their cot to sleep on the floor by the hearth, so that she might have a bed.

"I shall go on the morrow," she said. "Ye've been kind to me, Jock Nevins, and Mrs. Nevins be an angel from heaven, but I canna stay, whate'er ye might say. I can always get a place in a mill, I reckon."

But that very evening, Emma's tea was interrupted by a shout from outside the cottage door.

"Make haste, missy," Jock Nevins was calling. "Here be a boat'll give ye passage to Northwich, in return fer a bit o' help. Make haste, make haste. They want to make Hyde Bank Tunnel afore moorin'."

Emma started up, knocking over the stool on which she sat, the suckling babe on her knee. She had been giving it bits of bread, soaked in tea, while Mrs. Nevins fed the older ones.

"Gi' her to me," said Mrs. Nevins, holding out an arm. With the other hand, she was wrapping in a napkin the remainder of the loaf from the table. "Take this wi' ye," she said, thrusting the bread at Emma as she took the baby. "Dinna disremember yer bonnet. Be a good lass. Stop in when ye next come by."

"Oh, Mrs. Nevins, I thank ye," Emma cried, feeling the tears start in her eyes. Now the moment had come, she knew she did not truly want to leave this friendly place.

"Tush, lass," said Mrs. Nevins, pushing her toward the door. "Dinna take on. Ye'll find a good place, I know it, and be a credit to our charity."

Emma threw her arms around Mrs. Nevins, baby and all. Then she kissed the tops of the other children's heads and flew out the door. She called her thanks to Jock Nevins as she ran past him and down the steps to the lower bank.

Just coming out of the lock was a boat, painted blue and yellow. In the dusk, Emma could not make out the face of the boatman, but he held out his hand to her and pulled her on board as he passed by the bank where she stood.

Emma turned and waved to the tall figure beside the lock gate. She saw Mrs. Nevins, the baby in her arms and the two others clinging to her skirt, join him, and together they waved back at her.

She heard Jock Nevins's voice calling through the shadows.

"Fare thee well, missy," he cried.

# PAIN

IT WAS TWO DAYS TO NORTHWICH, two days and nights far longer than Emma could have imagined. For her help was not needed to drive the boatman's mule or steer the boat. The boatman had two sons. It was to nurse the boatman's wife, a rack of bones and tight-drawn skin who lay day and night on the cross bed.

"It be a canker o' the breast," said the boatman, his voice gruff. "She'll na suffer many more days, but the lads canna bear to see her so, and she needs a woman's care."

But Emma could scarcely bear to be in the cabin with the sick woman either. While Emma hovered helplessly near, now and again offering tea or gruel, bathing her forehead, changing the dirtied bedclothes, the woman clutched a windlass against the pain, and a sweetish, decaying smell rose from her. From time to time, a wrenching cry was torn from between her tight-pressed lips, and often her head turned from side to side as though she sought escape.

She seemed less a woman than a suffering animal, Emma thought, and it seemed to Emma that it would have been better for her if she were an animal. We'd na let a horse suffer so, she thought.

But deep in the second night, the woman's eyes cleared, and Emma heard her speak, a dry, gasping voice but lucid, urgent.

"Jem, be ye here? Jemmy, I want ye."

Emma stumbled from the side bed, where she had been nodding.

"I'll fetch him fer ye, missus. Hold fast."

The woman's head turned, and in the light of the candle burning on the table, Emma saw the gleam of her eyes.

"Mary? Is't Mary?"

"Nay, missus," Emma said, already at the cabin door. She slid back the hatch cover but paused a moment and turned back. "I be only Emma Deane. I dinna know yer Mary."

"Emma Deane?" The woman's voice was soft, tasting the name on her tongue.

"I be tendin' ye, missus, 'til ye be . . . well," Emma said.

The woman's great eyes burned, but she did not waste breath correcting what both of them knew was false.

"I thought ye be Mary," she said.

"Nay," Emma said again. "I'll fetch the mister fer ye."

She saw the woman's head move slightly before she turned to climb the step to the deck.

The boatman lay, wrapped in a blanket, atop the cabin roof. He was not sleeping, Emma saw, for he reared up on an elbow as her head emerged from the cabin.

"Be she . . ."

"She wants ye," Emma said, and stepped aside for him.

Emma waited, resting against the gunnel, and breathed deeply of the sweet night air. A cricket was fiddling in the grass of the bank. A night bird called from the trees.

She wondered that the boatwoman's sons, bundled in blankets beside the towpath, had not wakened at the stir of the boat, but, mayhappen they dinna *want* to hear, Emma thought, shivering as a cool wind lifted goose-flesh on her arms.

From below, she could hear the murmur of voices and an occasional sobbing cry, then, "Emma! Emma Deane!" in the boatman's choking voice.

Reluctantly, Emma climbed back down again into the warm stink of the cabin. The woman lay clutching the windlass, her lips drawn back from her teeth, her great eyes staring. Her husband hung over her, his tear-wet face desperate.

"Ha' she na had her drops?" he demanded of Emma.

"Aye, mister, but she canna keep them down,"

Emma said. "Mayhap if I bathe her forehead?"

She hurried to wring out a rag in the basin of water on the stove. The woman's soothing drops had done her no good for the last several hours, for she only vomited them or any bit of food or water that Emma had given her.

The man moved aside, so that Emma could touch the cloth to the strained white face. She squeezed a few drops of water onto the crusted lips, but the woman would not open them, only moved her head from side to side as though to say, leave me be. Her breath was loud and rasping, and Emma found herself breathing in time with her as she perched by the pillow and smoothed the furrowed forehead with her rag. The man knelt beside the bed, his head bowed onto the coverlet, and his shoulders shook.

Emma pulled the stale air into her lungs and painfully expelled it with the tortured breaths of the sick woman. She found herself crooning low in her throat, the way Nancy crooned to her baby.

Suddenly there was a silence. The woman had drawn a breath, but she did not exhale. Emma waited, her own breath held, as the seconds passed. Then, rattling, the woman's breathing began again. Now her eyes were closed. In. Out. In. Out. Emma counted the breaths. In. Out. In . . .

"Jemmy." The voice was soft, almost young sounding, and Emma saw that the woman's lips were moving.

The boatman raised his head.

In. Out. In . . .

"Na one day passed . . . that the joy . . . dinna outweigh . . . the pain . . ."

Slowly, the breath rattled out and was still.

Emma had seen death before. She had held in her arms Nancy's dead baby, but it seemed as though she held a doll, so little did she feel for it. She had seen a neighbor's husband brought home, broken and bleeding from a mill accident, but the neighbor's tears had not moved her. Long ago, dim now in her memory, she had looked on her mother and father, her brother and sister in their coffins, and had felt as senseless as they.

But this death hurt. She could feel the hurting in her chest. She felt dazed and sore and lost—as though someone lammed me in the head, she thought, lammed me hard in the heart.

While the silent boatman and his grieving sons brought the boat into Northwich the next day, Emma stayed below with the boatman's wife and wept. She wept as she bathed and dressed the poor diminished body for its coffin. She wept as she combed and braided the thin dry hair and as she pinned a gold brooch on the clean dark gown. She wept as she polished the woman's gold earrings and fastened them in her ears. She wept as she tidied the cabin, swept and polished and dusted so that the woman would not be shamed when they came to take her away. It seemed to Emma that her heart would break.

And I dinna know her hardly, she told herself in wonder. I have done more cryin' sin' I came to the cut than e'er I did afore, she thought. It seemed as though her heart had softened somehow, it was so easily pained.

Pain . . . and joy, the woman had said.

Mayhappen ye canna feel the one wi'out t'other, Emma thought, for she realized that she had felt joy as well. She had felt joy walking Rosie in the early morning dew. She had felt it evening times, cozy in the cabin, and when Mrs. Minshull spoke a rare word of praise, and when she, Emma, painted a flower so it looked like a flower, and when she listened to Birdie sing.

She thought of the old mill days—the long, deadening, leg-aching hours of standing by her reels with no idea in her head, but of baggin' time and her sup of bread or quittin' time and sleep.

She thought of Sundays when it had not been learning that had lured her to school, but the Sunday school treats of spiced cake and ale.

Then she thought of the satisfaction she had felt when she understood the working of the locks, the pleasure of teaching herself to paint, the pride when she mastered a bit of boatman's lore or boatwoman's craft.

Me heart ha' softened, to pain and joy both, Emma thought. She wept some more, for gladness.

# HINDRANCE

FROM A NORTHWICH WHARF, Emma watched the blue-and-yellow narrowboat move away from her. The boatman, his shoulders stooped, walked ahead beside his mule. His two sons stood behind the cabin, one of them with his hand on the tiller. The plain pine coffin rode in state in the hold.

They would be given precedence through the locks all the way to Ellesmere, the boatman had told Emma. "She were born on a boat by Burns Wood Bridge," the boatman had said, his eyes dry now and bleak. "She wished to be buried as near as may be. That be St. Mary's Church at Ellesmere, I reckon."

Emma had nodded, understanding the boatwoman's wish to spend all eternity near the cut where she was born. She, Emma, wanted never again to leave the canals—Fer I be a boatwoman now, she realized. A boatwoman wi'out a boat.

If Mr. Morton could not give her a post nor find her another boat, she would try the canal-side mills, she resolved.

So now, as the boat disappeared around a bend, Emma turned to ask the way to Isaac Morton's boatyard. A blue-bonneted woman pointed the direction.

It was a damp, gray evening. As Emma passed the warehouses and boatyards beside the canal, a faint mist rose from the water. The smell of wetness and rotted wood and tar was strong in her nose. She heard the quiet splash of the wake of a passing boat.

A row of narrowboats was moored beside Isaac Morton's dock. Emma saw an old man, sitting tailor-fashion before the cabin doors of a butty. He had a tray of paint pots near him on the stern.

It must be the old father what was poorly, Emma thought to herself, her heart sinking. She felt guilty for wishing the old man had not mended; if he were still sick, Mr. Morton might have need of a painter.

"Hallo," Emma said as she drew near. "Be ye Isaac Morton's old dad?"

The old man's white head turned, and he fixed her with a withering gaze.

"I be Isaac Morton. Young Isaac be me son," he said. "Who be ye?"

"Emma Deane," said Emma, feeling properly chastened. It seemed strange to think of Isaac Morton as young. His remembered face was as brown and wrinkled as his father's, only *his* hair was black.

"I be seeking t'other Mr. Morton," said Emma. "I did a job o' work fer him once."

The old man pursed his lips.

"Emma Deane," he said thoughtfully. "Ag Minshull's Emma Deane?"

Emma looked down at her dusty boots. She felt heat creep up her neck and into her face.

"Aye," she said, her voice low. "I did work fer Mrs. Minshull a time gone by."

The man unfolded his legs and stood, pulling himself up by a hand on the gunnel. From beneath her eyelashes, Emma saw him cup his hand around his mouth.

"Mrs. Minshull!" he hollered. "Mrs. Minshull, d'ye hear me? Yer lass has come back!"

Emma's heart stopped. Mrs. Minshull here? What was she doing in a boatyard? Why wasn't she out on the cut, getting the boat ahead?

"Oh, no!" Emma cried. "I dinna seek Mrs. Minshull. I dinna know she were here."

"Mrs. Minshull!" the old man shouted louder.

"Stow yer noise, Zac Morton," came Mrs. Minshull's voice from down the line of boats. "Ye'll wake the dead wi' yer din!"

Emma shot a startled glance in the direction of the voice and recognized the gaily painted stern of the *Cygnet* three boats away. Atop the cabin roof was a wicker bird-cage, and at the clatter of Mrs. Minshull's boots on the cabin step, a thrush began to trill.

"Birdie!" Emma cried in spite of herself, starting forward, then stopped in confusion, turned as though to flee, and was brought up short by her old mistress's imperious cry.

"Halt right there, ye scapegrace! I've a mind to gi' ye a taste o' me stick. Run off fer a bit of a holiday, did ye, wi' ne'er a by-yer-leave . . ." The old woman had heaved herself on deck and was hoisting her skirts to scramble onto the plank that led to the dock.

Emma turned to see her advancing and cringed from the rain of curses that came in her wake.

"Wand'rin' the byways at the mercy of any ne'er-do-well! What were ye thinkin' of? That's what I'd like to know. I'll be bound ye reckon ye can waltz right back and take yer old place, wi' ne'er a word spoken, do ye?"

Emma stood, her head bowed, and yet the old woman's voice seemed like birdsong, she was so glad to hear it. She felt the strong, skinny fingers close on her arm, and then she was being dragged down the dock toward the *Cygnet*. Mrs. Minshull never left off screeching all the way to the boat.

"Get yerself down to the cabin, ye slacker! I've a word to say to ye, and ye'll list whether yer willin' or no!" she cried when they were aboard. She shoved Emma toward the open cabin doors.

Emma stumbled down the step and into the warmth and coziness of the tiny orderly cabin. Mrs. Minshull was right behind her, and, as she edged past the hot stove, she felt the old woman's wiry arms close around her and found herself caught up in a breath-stopping hug. Then, so quickly she was not sure it had happened, Mrs. Minshull released her and pushed her onto the side bed, which, without its mattress, made a seat by the table.

"Set ye down there, an' hold yer tongue," Mrs. Minshull was raging. "Ye look most clemmed. I'll be bound ye've not supped this livelong day. What's to be done wi' the lass, that's what I'd like to know!"

Then she was clashing pot lids and rattling among her crockery, her back turned to Emma, her curses turned to muttering.

Emma sat, dazed, watching the jerky movements of Mrs. Minshull's black-clad arms and shoulders.

She be *glad* to see me, Emma thought, and her head spun with the thought, it was so unexpected. She be not angry, she be glad!

She caught a glimpse of Mrs. Minshull's face, as she turned to pull a trencher from its shelf. The wrinkled brown cheeks were wet, Emma saw, and the snapping black eyes glistened.

"Take off yer bonnet, ye vagabond!" Mrs. Minshull ordered in a muffled voice. "Make yerself useful, and lay the cloth. I'll be bound, I ne'er saw such a sloven!"

Emma pulled off her bonnet and hung it on its nail by the door. She reached into the drawer beneath the table and pulled out the familiar tablecloth, unshaking its pristine folds. On its surface she laid out their bowls and spoons and Mrs. Minshull's pewter saltcellar.

She be glad to see me, she kept repeating to herself, and her own eyes were wet.

Night fell quickly as they ate their simple tea of mutton's neck and carrots, peppered with Mrs. Minshull's lecturing. As soon as the dishes were scoured and put back in their places, Mrs. Minshull ordered Emma to bed.

The spare nightdress that had become Emma's own was in its accustomed drawer, washed and pressed and folded. As Emma undressed and put it on, Mrs. Minshull sat behind the curtain on the cross bed, finally silent. From time to time, Emma could hear her blow her nose on one of her immense pocket handkerchiefs. She heard the rustlings of her mattress as she too undressed and lay down to rest. Then, at last, the cabin was quiet, but for the occasional flutter of Birdie's wings against the wicker bars of his cage, brought in from the cabin roof and hung in its place from a hook in the ceiling. The boat moved gently, bumping against its neighbors, as another boat passed in the dark. Emma heard a towrope slide over the line of cabin roofs and then across their own. She heard the clop of an animal's hooves on the path beside the dock.

She thought of the blue-and-yellow boat, with its sad cargo, and wondered how late they would journey on their way to Ellesmere.

"'Tis late to be gettin' ahead," she said quietly in the darkness, and was startled by the sound of her voice.

For a moment, there was no answer. Then the cross bed mattress rustled, and, "Aye," Mrs. Minshull said.

Again, silence.

Emma had scarcely spoken since first Mrs. Minshull

had spied her on the dock, but now, in the warm dark and stillness, with Mrs. Minshull quiet at last, she remembered what Mrs. Nevins had asked.

*Did ye ne'er say what was in yer heart?*

Emma's heart was full to overflowing. Could she tell Mrs. Minshull what she was thinking? Would the old woman listen? Would she care?

"M-M-Mrs. Minshull?" It had come out in a whisper, and Emma was not certain the old woman had heard.

But, in a moment, came the soft "Aye" again.

"Mrs. Minshull, I be sorry fer leavin' ye wi' ne'er a word."

She heard a snort behind the curtain and rushed on. "It were me sister Nancy had me mithered. Her baby were sick, and there were only me wages to feed 'em. I thought, wi'out me . . . But, they dinna need me after all. They were managin' . . ."

There was no sound from behind the curtain.

"Do this signify ye'll have me back, Mrs. Minshull?" Emma whispered. "I'd work hard. Ye'd see. I'd ne'er run away again. . . ."

There was a long silence. Emma was beginning to think the old woman *was* angry with her when she heard a small sound. Then another. Then, Mrs. Minshull's voice, yet not quite Mrs. Minshull's voice either, it was so low and muffled.

"I know ye'd work hard, lass. Ye be a great hand fer workin', as steady and willin' a huffler as e'er I seed . . .

But . . . But I were an old fool to think I could get the boat ahead wi'out the mister. Hard as ye worked, we were na travelin' so far and so fast tha' we made a go o't. Folk be right. It do take a man's strength to get a boat ahead. E'en afore ye run off, I knew it. But I dinna want to know . . . I be sellin' *Cygnet* on the morrow and goin' to live on the bank."

"Sellin'!" Emma's voice was a cry. "Where'll ye live? *How'll* ye live? Ye said ye would na sell!"

"I have said rucks o' things in me life, lass!" Mrs. Minshull cried, her voice more like itself, Emma thought. "I have said rucks o' things I dinna mean!"

"But ye meant to keep the *Cygnet*," Emma said. "I heared ye tell that growlin' man that the mister would na sell, and ye would na neither. Besides, if ye sold, what'd become o' Rosie?"

"Ne'er ye mind Rosie!" shrilled Mrs. Minshull. "The knacker'll ne'er get Rosie while I've breath in me body. I be lookin' fer a boatman what needs a good animal. Rosie'll flourish, ne'er ye fear!"

Emma was shocked to silence. Sell Rosie to another boat? Steady as she was and trained to boats, Rosie was an old horse. Would there be another boatman who would want her? Or was the more likely buyer the knacker Mrs. Minshull protested against? She'd ne'er sell Rosie to the knacker fer horse meat and glue! Would she?

She be flinchin', Emma thought with a sick feeling in the pit of her stomach. I ne'er would have thought Mrs. Minshull would flinch.

# . . . AND JOY

WHEN THE CABIN WINDOWS WERE JUST beginning to lighten to circles of lacy gray, Emma at last heard the whistling snore of Mrs. Minshull. The old woman had not slept most of the night, Emma could tell from the restless rustling of her mattress and her occasional weary sigh. But Emma had not slept either. At least, not much. She kept asking herself if Mrs. Minshull would have flinched if she'd known she had Emma to depend on. She could not help thinking it was her fault the old woman had despaired.

It be me duty to save the *Cygnet*, Emma thought.

All night Emma's head had whirled with mad plans. They could take on another huffler. . . . But a real huffler would expect wages and be another mouth to feed besides. They could hire on with a boat company, who would find them cargoes and pay them for the hauling. . . . But was not this a worse humiliation than selling up?

And what company would want a boat crewed by an old woman and a girl and pulled by an elderly horse? They could find a moorage beside a green meadow where Rosie could graze, and Emma would take work in a mill to buy their food. . . . But where could Rosie be stabled in the fast-approaching cold weather? And would mill wages suffice for stabling and oats, much less food for two people, even if Emma could find such a job?

Where would Mrs. Minshull go when the boat had been sold?

Where would Rosie go if a boatman could not be found to buy her?

And where would Emma go?

Now, silently, Emma raised herself to a sitting position. Silently, she pulled on petticoat and gown and felt for her boots. Holding the boots in one hand, silently she tiptoed to the cabin doors, and inch by inch, she slid back the hatch. The cool, damp air of morning touched her fevered face. Emma eased herself onto the deck and closed the doors and hatch cover behind her. She could hear the steady whistle of Mrs. Minshull's snore. Birdie had not stirred.

Emma tiptoed across the plank to the dock and knelt to lace on her boots. Then she squatted beside the boat, arms hugging her knees, and thought.

A new day was streaking the sky with light. In its cool illumination, it seemed to Emma that her frantic mind slowed. It began to move quietly from thought to thought, no longer spinning dizzily, but turning over each idea in the orderly way that Mrs. Minshull had taught her to tidy the cabin.

There mun be somewhat I can do, Emma thought. Somewhat . . .

And then, as the first clear ray of sunlight pierced the sky above the horizon, Emma leapt to her feet, her heart pounding, and ran to find Isaac Morton.

His cottage was behind the boatyard, facing a little lane. Flowers touched by frost drooped beside the garden wall—roses, their orange hips swollen, pinks and sweet williams and heartsease, draggling their last limp blooms.

Emma pulled open the little gate and ran up the flagstone path to the door. Inside, as she paused to raise her hand, she heard voices and the clink of tableware. She knocked.

A comely woman with cheeks pink from the fire opened the door. She tilted her head to one side.

"Ye'd be Emma Deane, I reckon," she said before Emma had found her voice.

"Emma Deane, come in. Come in!" rang Isaac Morton's voice.

"Ye be up wi' the birds this day," called old Mr. Morton.

They were sitting on the settle beside the hearth—both Isaac Mortons—eating their porridge. Side by side, they looked as like as two peas in a pod, thought Emma, save for the shock of white hair on the elder.

"I have come to beg a favor," Emma said, stepping inside the door Mrs. Morton held open.

"We'll listen," said old Mr. Morton, his eyes wary.

Suddenly Emma's elation drained away. It was but another mad idea, she thought. They would laugh her to scorn.

"Well?" said old Mr. Morton impatiently.

"M-M-Mrs. Minshull be agoin' to sell the *Cygnet*," Emma faltered.

Both Mr. Mortons nodded, their eyes solemn.

"Aye," they murmured together.

"Jeb Hawkins'll be here 'round noontide wi' the papers," said old Mr. Morton.

"He'll gi' a fair price," comforted young Isaac.

"But the poor ol' woman'll be lost wi'out her boat," said Mrs. Morton. "She have lived aboard it sin' she were a bride."

"Aye," the Isaac Mortons murmured, nodding.

"If there were somewhat we could do . . . ," said young Isaac Morton.

"But there be!" cried Emma, taking heart. "Ye could sell me some water cans an' nose tins an' coal bins an' such, like what ye paint fer the boats. Some plain ones straight from the tinsmith."

"O' course, lass," said old Mr. Morton. "But why?"

"So's ye can paint 'em and sell 'em again yerself!" cried young Isaac Morton, jumping up from the settle. He began to pace in excitement.

"I canna pay ye 'til I have painted 'em and sold 'em," Emma explained. "That be the favor. Ye'd have to gi' 'em me on trust."

"Ye *could* sell 'em, once ye'd painted 'em," young Isaac Morton said consideringly. His eyes gleamed, and a smile was beginning to light his face. "Ye could sell 'em fer a sight more than ye'd pay us."

Emma was nodding. She could feel an answering smile breaking on her own face.

"D'ye think it'd be enough?" she said. "I'd do the paintin' evenin's and off times, so's we could get the boat ahead as well. Would it be enough to make a go o't? Enough fer Rosie's stablin' an' the fees and food and the like?"

"Aye, wi' what the boat earns, it would!" exclaimed both Mr. Mortons at once. Mrs. Morton was hugging herself delightedly, and the old man was up and pacing beside his son. He turned and clapped young Isaac Morton on the shoulder.

"It would be!" he cried again, and they turned to her as one man, beaming.

"Folks'd vie fer goods painted by a hand as steady and clever as yourn," young Isaac Morton said, and his father chimed in.

"Ye'd ha' a good business in no time, I'll wager, fer I'd be well shut o' the little nigglin' jobs. 'Tis all I can do to keep up wi' paintin' the boats."

"Oh, Mr. Morton," Emma breathed.

Now young Isaac Morton was pounding his father on the back.

"Oh, Mr. Morton!" Emma cried to him too.

"I cotched ye!" came a voice from the open doorway.

Emma whirled to see Mrs. Minshull advancing on her, her wrinkled face red and furious.

"Ye thought ye could get away wi'out sayin' farewell!" Mrs. Minshull was crying. "Well, I cotched ye this time, me lass. Ye can ne'er again pull the wool o'er Ag Minshull's eyes!"

She clutched Emma's arm and shook her violently. Emma's teeth rattled in her mouth, and the room swung crazily before her eyes.

"Aggie!"

Emma felt the clawlike hand release as Mrs. Minshull was dragged from her. The Isaac Mortons had grabbed her, one on each side, and old Mr. Morton was shouting.

"Aggie, get ahold o' yerself. The lass were na leavin' ye. She were savin' ye, if ye'll be still fer a minute and listen. She were savin' yer worthless hide and yer worn-out boat and yer useless animal, and this be the way ye thank her! I'd na blame her fer leavin' ye now!"

Mrs. Minshull had fallen silent.

They plumped her down on a chair and stepped back, and old Mr. Morton shook his head, frowning.

"Ye be a daft old woman, Ag Minshull. Ye dinna know when folk care fer ye, and ye canna shut yer maw long enough fer them to tell ye so!"

Mrs. Minshull blinked and stroked the hairs on her chin.

"She were na leavin'?" she said.

"I were na!" cried Emma, rubbing her arm where the old woman had grasped it.

"I dinna hurt ye?" Mrs. Minshull said, her voice shamed.

"Nay," said Emma. "Ye ne'er have hurt me. 'Tis me what's hurt ye . . ."

"Nay, lass, nay . . ."

"But ye be flinchin', Mrs. Minshull, and it be me fault!" Emma knelt before the old woman's chair and put out her hand.

"Flinchin'? Ag Minshull flinchin'?" For a moment the old woman looked irate. Then the fire went from her eyes. "Aye," she said. "I be. But the fault be na yourn, lass. Na yourn at all, but me own, fer thinkin' a slow old woman an' a slow old horse could get a boat ahead."

Mrs. Minshull took Emma's hand in hers, and the strength and warmth of it gave Emma courage to say, "I want to stay wi' ye, and mayhappen there be a way to make a go o't after all."

It was soon told. Mrs. Minshull sat holding Emma's hand and shaking her head. When Emma and the Mortons had fallen silent, she looked around at them, fixing each with her piercing gaze.

"The boat would na be sold?"

They shook their heads.

"Nor Rosie?"

Again they shook their heads.

Then she looked at Emma, and Emma saw in her fierce look that betraying glitter.

"Ye would na leave me, lass?"

Emma patted the work-worn hand holding hers.

"Nay, Mrs. Minshull." She remembered what Mrs.

Nevins had said about saying what was in her heart. "I be fond o' ye, Mrs. Minshull," Emma said softly, "and I think ye be fond o' me."

Emma gave Rosie's harness a last neatening pat and looked over at the *Cygnet*, which the Mortons had walked down the dock, away from the other boats. A cold sun sparkled on the wind-roughened water, but Emma, in her tied-on shawl, did not feel it. She was watching Mrs. Minshull nod to young Isaac Morton, who cast off the last rope. Mrs. Minshull looked forward to Emma and cupped her hand to her mouth.

"Get on, lass! Be ye waitin' fer the millennium? We've a cargo to find an' load!"

Emma smiled and clucked to Rosie. The horse leaned into her collar, her great brown eyes fixed trustingly on Emma, and Emma felt, as Rosie felt them, the resistance of the boat and the sudden release as it floated free of the bank. She knew Mrs. Minshull was leaning on the tiller to bring *Cygnet* to midstream.

"Fare thee well, Mrs. Minshull!" Emma heard the Mortons calling from the dock. "Fare thee well, Emma Deane!"

"I'll have some orders fer ye, the next time ye come by," cried young Isaac Morton.

"And a dish o' tea," cried his wife.

"And I'll show ye a castle scheme what be good fer water cans," cried old Mr. Morton.

"Tell Jeb Hawkins he mun wait fer another time!" cackled Mrs. Minshull. "Tell 'im Ag Minshull still be a mulish old woman. Tell 'im her huffler be right mulish too!"

Emma laughed out loud. She turned to wave at the Mortons, who stood in a line on the dock. Mrs. Morton was touching her eyes with her apron, and the Mr. Mortons, father and son, raised hands in a salute.

Emma straightened her shoulders and marched forward.

She could use her walking time, she thought, to plan the painting of the boat ware stacked in the hold. She had in mind a rose design for water cans. She'd twine the roses 'round the spouts and handles as the Mortons' garden roses twined about their wall, only Emma's roses would be spring blossoms, just opening, their colors fresh and bright.

Wi' a dew drop here and there, Emma thought, as though the roses be cryin' fer joy.

That made her think of Nancy. The next time they went through Macclesfield, Emma would take her a little wooden cricket for Benny to sit on by the hearth. She would make it as blue as Benny's eyes, she thought, with a pattern of flowers on the seat.

Beside her, Rosie snuffled in her nose tin, and from the cabin roof, Birdie trilled. Emma turned her head to catch a glimpse of Mrs. Minshull's black bonnet riding proudly above the stern. The cocky set of it, its flouncing ruffled by the wind, put Emma in mind of the flowers she would paint on Benny's stool.

Heartsease, she thought.

# ❧ GLOSSARY ❧

The author is indebted to the nineteenth-century novel *Mary Barton* by Mrs. Elizabeth Gaskell for many of the colorful words and expressions peculiar to Victorian working folk that are used in this book. Others were gleaned from Flora Thompson's memoir, *Lark Rise to Candleford*; and, of course, English canal folk had a vocabulary of their own. Some words whose meaning may be obscure to the modern American reader are listed below.

**baggin' time**  a twenty-minute break in the mill worker's afternoon for tea and bread

**bank, the**  canal folk referred to people who did not live on boats as "livin' on the bank"

**bollard**  a sturdy post on a wharf or at a lock or tunnel used for holding mooring ropes

**bugger off**  desert, leave suddenly

**clemmed**  hungry

**cozen**  deceive

**cygnet**  a young swan; the name of Mrs. Minshull's narrowboat

**dateless**  crazed

**dolly (dollyin')**  stir clothes in a laundry tub

**dree**  long and tedious

**fettle (fettlin')**  put in order, tidy

**fortnight**  a period of two weeks

**frab**  worry or pick at someone

**gloppened**  amazed

**huffler**  a narrowboat crew member

**lam**  beat, hit, strike

**mither**  trouble, perplex

**narrowboat**  boat designed for British "narrow" canals, powered in the eighteenth, nineteenth, and first half of the twentieth centuries by horses; traditional narrowboats are approximately seven feet wide and up to seventy feet long with a cabin ten feet long and five feet high

**nesh**  tender

**side**  put in order, tidy

**sop**  bread steeped in boiling water, then strained and sugared

**stuff gown**  gown made of woolen cloth

**togs**  clothes

**treacle**  molasses